All Souls

All Souls

Christine Schutt

Harcourt, Inc.

Orlando   Austin   New York   San Diego   London

www.HarcourtBooks.com

Library of Congress Cataloging-in-Publication Data
Schutt, Christine, date.
All souls/Christine Schutt.—1st ed.
p.   cm.
1. Private schools—Fiction.   2. High school students—Fiction.
3. Female friendship—Fiction.   4. New York (N.Y.)—Fiction.   I. Title.
PS3569.C55555A45   2008
813'.54—dc22   2007032814
ISBN 978-0-15-101449-1

Text set in Bell MT Std
Designed by Linda Lockowitz

Printed in the United States of America
First edition
A C E G I K J H F D B

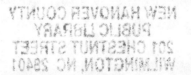

To my students, of course

Contents

All Souls

The Girl No One Knows

Fathers

Mr. Dell, in his daughter's room, stuck his face into the horn of a stargazer lily, one of a . . . one of a . . . must have been a dozen, and he breathed in and said wasn't that something. And wasn't it: the pileup of cards, a stuffed bear, a bouquet of balloons, a banner, a bed jacket, books on tape.

We love you, Astra! The chorus to his daughter was always the same, and he, too, said the same, but he did not look at her famished face, did not meet her eye, did not take her hand; he wheezed out only so much cheer. "That party at the Mortons'" was how he started. Mr. Dell stood between his daughter's bed and the window and described what he could of the Mortons' party. "I've been to Suki's before, Dad." Okay, he had forgotten, so other things, then. Not far into the kickoff fund-raiser, the host had stood on a piano bench to say he was not sorry to be so poorly acquainted with the parents gathered, but he expected to know a lot about everyone by the end of the school year when the money for the senior gift was raised. "Then Mr. Morton expected he would never see any of us again."

"That sounds like Suki's dad."

"Suki's mother is funny."

The room Suki's father had spoken in was a very big, cream-colored box of a room, a cake box, a hatbox, something large and expensive. Mr. Dell described the party to his daughter in the way Grace would have described it: how things looked and sounded, the gurgle of civility among designing adults. He described what it felt like to be known as the parent of such a child, his own, his only, his best, bright addition.

"Dear, dear Astra, how are you feeling?" he asked now.

"Daddy," Astra said, and she smiled when she told him how corny he was.

He told his daughter who had come to the Mortons'. Mrs. Forestal was there, so Mr. Forestal was not. Mr. and Mrs. Van de Ven, Mrs. Abiola, the Cohens, and Mr. Fratini were there. "I talked a lot to Alex's mother—is that woman crazy? The Johnsons were not in attendance. The headmistress, Miss Brigham, was there for a short speech, and she asked after you—everyone there asked after you, darling. Everyone sends love." Then he remembered that the Johnsons were in Europe meeting somebody royal.

Astra said, "The Johnsons have expensive fights that end with new jewels."

The Mortons' apartment was all bloody mahogany and damask. Crystal chandeliers, those plinking rainbows, were hanging everywhere. Double sconces, elaborate molding, herringbone floors. The caterers were using monogrammed family silver. The word *expansive* came to mind, or a three-tiered cake on a crystal stand, a monument in buttercream frosting, swags of sugar violets, silver dots. That was the equivalent dessert to the Mortons' apartment as far as Mr. Dell was concerned. He looked at Astra again and saw how tired she was; her eyelids looked swollen as if she had been crying, and perhaps she had cried. He hadn't been here for all the tests; he was at work.

"I wish I could be hungry," Astra said. She shut her eyes.

Good night, ladies, good night, ta, ta, or however it went. Mr. Dell thought literature should be a consolation, but what he most often remembered did not comfort him. He did not have his wife's gift, Astra's inheritance from Grace for hope and serenity. Sick as his little girl was, she yet lay hopeful of recovery—fearful, too, at times, at times overwhelmed, given to deep, jagged sobs, and yet . . . she was sick and in pain on a sad floor in the hospital, and yet she seemed to feel his terror, his sorrow, and she consoled him by being mostly mild, sleepy, quiet. Most of the time when he visited, she slept and slept. She grew smaller.

Again he asked and again, day after day, "How do you feel?"

Better. Not well. Sick. Hurting. Hurting a lot. Here is where it hurts the most. Look at what they did.

Why was it hard to look when he had already looked into disaster, into the broken face of his beautiful wife in a bag on a gurney? Yes, he remembered saying to the figures standing behind him—a row of janitors, a man with a mop at attention was that who? Policemen? Morticians? *Yes. My wife. This is Grace Walker Dell, yes. My wife.*

What business had Grace there on that street at that hour? Why had she not been home, but she was saving money looking for a new lamp on Bowery. He wanted her here with him at this other, terrible bedside. He should not have to be alone.

Mothers

Theta Kovack called First Wok and ordered garlic chicken, noodles, soup. Two Cokes. Marlene, at her ear, said, "General Tsao's! Get General Tsao's!" But Theta said, "Aren't you on a diet?" and she scuffed off her shoes and unbuttoned her blouse. The twenty she extracted from her purse felt damp. "For when the guy comes," she said, holding out the money. She let her skirt slip down her hips as she walked to her room and shimmied out of work. Of course, she didn't want to see herself, but she saw herself, or parts of herself, her belly rucked by the band of her slip, an angry redness she rubbed at. Glad she had not gone to the Mortons' party arrived wrongly dressed. Now the damp smell was surely hers, and nothing of Dr. Bickman's office—the minty wintergreen of mouthwash, the cleansing alcohol, the doilies on the trays of tools—remained. A subway with a few stops and a three-block walk was all it had taken to grease Theta's face.

A Daughter

Miss Wilkes, undressing at home, sniffed the bitter smell at the underarms of her turtleneck and said, "My god!" She sniffed again. When did her sweat turn so peculiarly acrid? The face she saw in the mirror, her own, seemed still a girl's, not a teacher's, but the stink of her was something awful, old. True, the girls themselves were not always so fresh. Edie Cohen, in her usual rush, liked to announce she hadn't showered. The girls said, "Keep your arms down. Stay away!" But the girls got up close to each other and examined each other and were amused or mockingly repelled by what they sometimes found. "Want an Altoid?" Good girls mostly, polite, they

offered her Skittles and mints, whatever they had se-
creted—and she allowed. Miss Wilkes said, "Yeah, I
would like," and she took her favorite colors. They got
up close for her to pick and seemed startled at what
they saw. What did they see? But they were never so familiar as to fix her. They would let her go through a
class smudged rather than say, "Miss Wilkes, you've got
ink on your chin." Only Lisa Van de Ven had stopped
her, had said, "Wait." Lisa it was who had tucked in the
label of her shirt, who had said, "Miss Wilkes," holding
out a box of Kleenex. Lisa Van de Ven, Lisa. Miss
Wilkes was on the bed with the weight of her hand between her legs.

Mothers

In a corner apartment with a southwestern view of Park
Avenue's islands bedded with begonias, glossy begonias,
Suki Morton's mother held the phone in one hand and
a drink in the other and heard her daughter's screed
against that fat Dr. Meltzer and his chem class labs. "He
keeps us late. He piles on the homework. We're seniors,
for god's sake. We're under a lot of stress as it is. I hate
Dr. Meltzer."

Mrs. Morton could not come up with an expression.
Dr. Meltzer was a name attached to a fat man who
smelled like the movies. Buttery and smoky at the same

time. Butter-yellow teeth. Short-sleeved shirt, pocket protector, high waist, and waddle. Surely encountered in the movies but a teacher to be found in a public school, never one like Siddons. Mrs. Morton hung up the phone and said, "I never liked science."

Ten blocks south, Suki's best friend, Alex, was watching cheese melt over chips. She was talking to herself, rehearsing a college interview, saying that what she loved about this college was there were more boys than girls, better parties, good drugs. Alex was saying her ambition was to be the most famous party girl the school had ever known, and she knew what she was doing, and she could meet this goal.

Car Forestal twisted utensils through food she had mashed to look like war salvage, drought gruel, rancid scraps from boarding school. She was at the orphanage and eating with her baby "pusher," the tiny silver spade from her godmother. Car pushed and smoothed and rearranged the food; she made patterns.

"Look, Carlotta, if you're not going to eat it, at least stop this baby business. Not everything on your plate has to be mashed." Mrs. Forestal said she simply could not sit for hours and play the warden, and she pronounced Car's manners repugnant and left the table. Car excused herself elaborately—"May I please"—and made answer, "Why of course, my dear," and the girl left her plate of food that no longer looked like food and went to her room and drank water.

Sarah Saperstein and her father were talking about global warming, and Edie Cohen—Dewdrop to her father—was listening to her father talk about her older brother, Jake, the pride of the family, a sophomore at MIT who was making computer programs for Intel or Extel or Ontel, some techno-sounding company that had a *tel* to it. Edie Cohen's brother was one of the reasons she worked so hard; she had his career to live up to no matter what her parents said. Her parents said they didn't care what grades she got as long as Dewdrop could say she had given her all.

Ufia, the black princess, was eating chickpeas and telling her mother she didn't think Mr. O'Brien saw the racist significance of the Dickinson poem, at least not the way she did. "Just think of the term," she said. "'White Election.' Could anything be more obvious?"

Kitty Johnson had come home after seven from advisory with Mr. O'Brien, and her head ached. Kitty said it was a migraine-order headache, and she told the housekeeper she was going to bed. "I'm not going to be 'up to nothing' in my room, as you say. I won't be phoning anyone. I don't do that, anyway. I just don't want any dinner."

———

What other conversations were there? Was there still talk of the Dells, Astra Dell especially? Was the subject of her cancer old, or simply avoided because it diminished all the other griefs a healthy person felt? Here was a body dangerously sick: Astra Dell, that pale girl from the senior class, the dancer with all the hair, the red hair, knotted or braided or let to fall to her waist, a fever, and she consumed.

CHF

The sofa Car sat on was smooth as a mushroom and so plumply overstuffed that no indented evidence of her remained when she stood up; in fact, there was no evidence of anyone's passing through her father's apartment, and she could only imagine the swaying enormity of the cleaning lady, who was so thorough in her work that the slats of light through the blinds seemed dustless. Here all was sealed, unscented, unused, unmarked, yet the clock was wound and keeping time. Her father's drawers were empty; his closet, locked. Car had a key to her father's apartment, and this, she supposed, was enough, was a lot really, and meant she could wander and phone as she would, as she had and did last week, this week, any week, and because her father's number was unlisted and her mother didn't know it, Car was inaccessible. *That man!* was all her mother said. That man,

Car's father, impeccably pressed and pleated, was surely in handsome company. *Dearest girl.* He wrote the occasional postcard that took weeks to get across the ocean. *Dearest wren. Today in the Galleria Borghese, William stood in front of the Bernini and wept. You know the statue. Daphne breaking into branches.* Her father was a character in a Henry James novel. Car lit up another cigarette and ashed it on the table.

Marlene

Marlene picked her nose and sent what she found in it flying across her room. She was a dirty girl, she knew that much, and whatever the girls in school suspected her of—stealing, farting, lying—was true. The slut part was not true, although she wished it were, but all the dirty parts—yes, she was that girl. Look at her messy room, the unresolve of such disorder. She had no ambition but to dizzy herself into absence. Smoking cigarettes helped. The nights when her mother came home and went straight to bed saying her feet were swollen, those nights Marlene often shamed herself into high feeling. She flashed her ass in the bright windows of the living room; she pulled her cheeks apart; she said, *Kiss my a-hole;* she said, *Eat me.* Ugly expressions she used as she would spit, and she picked at herself and made worse scabs. But who could see this now in the soft light of her bedroom? She wrote to Astra Dell and chewed her nails to a bloody quick she blotted on the draft of her letter . . . *Dear Astra.* She meant what she wrote, the *dear* part. Of all the girls in her class, only Astra Dell had ever been genuinely kind to her and was, yes, was dear to her, and now Marlene was in a position to help Astra. To help Astra Dell! To be her friend as no other. *I have never shared more than a hello nod or a smile with you, but the one time I saw you cry, I wanted to share those tears with you. I am thinking of you,* which was purely the truth. Marlene was thinking of Astra and rumors of scorching treatments being used to cure her. Marlene wrote three pages, single-spaced, telling Astra about stupid things, school, Miss F. *She either just sits there and waits for you to have some trigono-metric moment or tells you that she cannot believe that you don't know it.* Marlene's letters were filled with what-ever she had overheard in the senior lounge, for she had found a place there for herself in the lounge. Alex began laughing hysterically over nothing in chemistry, and Dr. Meltzer kicked her out of the class. Marlene often sat in the corner of the lounge leaned up against the lockers, and from there she listened in, took notes, copied stories, scribbled, drew flowers. Alex was mak-ing a video of the senior experience, but Marlene was writing it all down for the sick girl.

Marlene wrote to Astra about her yearbook page. Marlene Kovack, *Last Heard Saying: Nothing.* Who wrote that? Marlene had some ideas—Suki Morton and Alex Decrow. Some joke.

But there's always got to be one person to hate in every class, right? Marlene wrote to Astra: *Expect to see Alex's movie. She's shoving her camera into everyone's face.* Even Marlene's, of course. Marlene had been asked to look into the camera and say something to Astra. Marlene, watching from her corner, had said, "Catch me in action," and then held as still as she could, hardly seeming to breathe. Alex filmed some girls from below because, as Alex said, the angle was so fucking freaky, possibly original; the way a little kid sees the world is mostly oily, prickly legs. Marlene believed Alex wanted everyone to look ugly. That was school for Marlene, an ugly ongoing movie, but now suffering had another meaning, real suffering led to real death. *Dear Astra, I hope to see you even before you get this letter*, and she did hope to see Astra; this was the truth.

Siddons

Dembroski was checking off attendance in senior class meeting.

Alex Decrow?

Edie Cohen—sick.

Marlene Kovack—

Suki Morton?

Later Mrs. Dembroski wondered at the suspended notation for Marlene Kovack; she couldn't account for her own indecision on the matter. Where was Marlene on Wednesday?

Unattached

Anna Mazur sat near the end of the bed and watched Astra's breathing because everything else she looked at was hospital-like, too white and too clean, bandaged, tubed, needled, starched, so that the rise and fall of Astra's breathing in the bed was what she watched, the way she might watch a clock, as if the visit could be hurried by such attention, but her time at the hospital was like all time at the hospital and slow! A nurse came in and pinged the IV sac, and later the nurse came back and said, "Still sleeping is she?" and Anna wondered at the sameness of hospital talk, remembering her brother Mitchell in a cold room where he slept and slept away what little time was left. The unfairness of things. Anna Mazur knew Astra from the English Speaking Union's Shakespeare contest. "You see me, Lord Bassanio, where I stand." Anna had never been Astra's teacher; she had only stepped in to coach when, last year, Miss Hodd was out and Astra had needed help to prepare for the contest. Anna liked the girl very much and wished she had taught her, wished she had been a favorite, but Anna had never been anyone's favorite. (She was no Tim Weeks.) Maybe in a different school or another profession, she might be valued more. Oh, she had been liked as a teacher, yes, even well liked on occasion, but nobody's best, nobody's favorite. She had been three years at Siddons and had never seen Tim Weeks's apartment. Anna stared at the blanketed rise of the sick girl's feet. She thought Astra's toes would break off if she touched them, and so she backed out of the room in good-bye, glad to be gone and down so many floors and into the unseasonably flushed and humid yellow air. She shivered to be alive, but the unfairness of things—criminals turning on the spit of their crimes, the crooked and maimed and unspeakably wicked thrumming with health while the innocent died—saddened Anna, and she called Tim Weeks once outside.

He said, "Why don't you come over?" And when she didn't answer, he said, "Take a taxi. I'm not really as far as you think."

She didn't know where to sit once she was in his apartment. The couch was serving as a table; stacks of magazines and newspapers and books took up its length, and the chair under a reading lamp was clearly Tim's, so that the only other possible chair was the beanbag in the corner. "From somebody's youth," he said, "probably mine."

She moved around the room. She looked at the

books on his shelves: biographies—Ernest Hemingway, Adlai Stevenson, Frank Lloyd Wright—and in a cleared space a picture of a dour little girl and another picture of her, younger by years, smiling on a lawn in a skirted bathing suit. "My niece. My sister's children. They live with the folks in Ohio. The little boy's name is Ted. He's six, I think, or he may be seven." The little boy was cuter than his sister, freckled, a little like Tim. "He looks like you," she said.

"I'm flattered," he said. "I'm glad. I've got beer and beer. What would you like?"

"Nothing."

"Really?"

But she joined him in a beer, clinking bottles as he moved his chair closer to the couch, remarking that they had more than Siddons in common; they were both from the Midwest. Yes, he said. He knew that, and Tim was glad she had called, had come; he had been wondering about her visit to Astra Dell.

"Yes," she said.

"So?"

"The girl slept the whole time. She opened her eyes when I first got there, and she may have seen me. I don't know. The nurse said she would tell Astra I'd been there." Anna drank and shrugged her shoulders, said she was tired. She said, "So," said, "Nothing much to say except I'm depressed."

He took the beer from her hand and kept her hand in his and looked at her in that Tim Weeks way he had, and he was adorable again.

She said, "Well, I'm not suffering, am I? I came here, didn't I? I'm sitting with you and drinking beer and playing the sad sack when what do I have to be sad about?"

"Don't be so hard on yourself. You have reason to be sad. There's something wrong about a child gravely ill. There's the memory of your brother."

"You think they could fix it by now. You think they'd know more."

"Next time maybe I should go with you," and he let go of her hand.

"I'm not being hard on myself. I was glad for an excuse to call you."

He smiled. He talked about quiet experiences and how it helped to see a lot of foliage from the windows of his apartment. "Look," he said, and she did, and she saw the leaves on the cherry trees were small and ovate and a yellow-red that looked edible.

"I like where you live."

CHF

By the time Car got to the hospital, visiting hours were almost over, but Astra was awake, and when the girls saw each other, they cried. Astra was hooked to ma-

chinery and fenced off behind a castered table, so that
Car stood aloof and cried. The words for what they
were feeling were ordinary, familiar words, and Car was
sorry to say them. Even the language behind her silence
was worn and uninspired and whapped the way balloons did without surprise or weight. And what had she
brought to show Astra? Old photos, the colors too
bright; the beach, a hurtful white against the blue of
everything else. Astra in a tented costume and Car in a
bathing suit, and both of them laughing at Car's father,
who had taken pictures then. The girls eating lobster.
Car asleep in the hammock. The girls older and eating
lobster. Sweet peas whimsically tangled on tepeed trel-
lises, and hydrangeas, so heavy headed from a rain, they
flopped on the lawn as if playing dead. Pictures of the
front of the house swept and raked. Thor, more of Thor,
this time with his bone. Kayaks far out in the bay.
"That's us," Car said. "Remember? That was the same
day we saw Will Bliss and met his friend from Taft. Remember?" Astra remembered. There had been a party
on the beach, a bonfire. Astra said, "Will Bliss, just the
name. You have to love him. Besides, what's wrong with
looking cute all the time and being the favorite friend of
little children?"

Car smiled. "What was that song those boys were
singing?"

What was it? But Car didn't remember what it was
or what she was going to say next, and she opened the

present she had brought for Astra while Astra watched: a bracelet, light as the cotton it was swaddled in, from Cartier, thin as a string, a silver bracelet beaded with silver beads. Astra's mouth opened in a kind of smile, her tears looked milky, and Car was ashamed to look at Astra and turned her attention to the upright row of cards.

"All your cards!" Car said. "This one," and she opened and read and put it behind another card. "Lisa Van de Ven has the neatest, fattest handwriting. *'Dear Astra . . . at least you're escaping Mr. O'Brien's first-period Monday class . . . ugh. I'm sure you're happy about that. And you'll be able to catch up on the sleep . . .'* Lisa is such a bore." Car took up another and read aloud: *" 'Remember the chorus trip when we stayed up all night and talked about EVERYTHING!!!?'* Who is this from? Edie, I should have known. And Alex of AlexandSuki, what did they have to say? *'I miss you a lot, and I know so many people have said that to you, but I know that you know that coming from me . . .'* Alex is so crazy. You know she's making a video about the senior experience? She thinks it'll look good on her applications." The rest of the cards Car read to herself, and when she turned back to Astra, her best friend's eyes were shut. They were shut and her face settled in a way more final than before, and Car knew she was asleep. Someone rapped at the door; visiting hours were over; it was time. True enough, the room had darkened. The corridor, too, was asleep, and the nurses' station empty, and the doors along the hall were half shut on screened-off beds, and nowhere was there music or TV, only the nurse on spongy soles, moving just ahead, checking on the darkness from room to room, saying to Car as they walked down the corridor, "She's looking pretty good, your friend."

"Was that good?" and when the nurse didn't answer right away, Car said that maybe she could come tomorrow. Maybe, yes, she should come. Tomorrow. Tomorrow was school again. *Folio* meeting. She had AP calculus to do. No frees tomorrow except lunch. No lunch tomorrow. Tomorrow no food, nothing, only water.

Siddons

Edie Cohen explained right speech involved abstinence from "lying, telling tales, harsh language, and frivolous talk." In the first skit at morning meeting, three girls were talking, and as a fourth approached, one girl said to the others, "Don't let her join our group." In the second skit, four girls were talking and after one of them had left, the others spoke behind her back: "She is a drag. I wish she wouldn't follow us."

In the third skit, four girls were talking and then one of them walked to a pile of book bags and took something that was clearly not hers. When later she had the opportunity to confess, she lied: "I didn't take anything."

Marlene played the student who said, "Don't let her join our group," a line she had heard: Lisa Van de Ven, eighth grade, middle school. The jittery disconnect and suddenness of middle school: breasts and stinks. Rumors, boys, dances. The boys froze some fatty's bra and waved it like a flag in Frost Valley.

Unattached

Anna Mazur did not like Tim Weeks's apartment as much as she liked her own. Hers had a view of the East River. Every time she opened the front door to her apartment, she walked toward the restlessness, the choppy, mostly dun-colored or black shivering river as seen from the picture window, a view that powerfully affirmed the rightness of her relocation from Michigan. Hers was a postwar building, and the windows were modern with wide panes—she needed to get them washed—and the rent for her apartment was a matter of its view and the floor, the twelfth floor, a junior one-bedroom, which meant not quite a studio, not quite a one-bedroom, but five hundred square feet of living space for a large chunk of what she made every month. Her mother had asked more than once, "How much can you save living in a city like New York?" Money for

Anna, at age twenty-eight, was not the point; she had wanted sophistication and experience. The private school in Michigan where she first taught had a B reputation, or so said her cousin, the lawyer—and who better than the lawyer to know? In Anna's eighth-grade classroom at Siddons, early in the teaching year, she had one day come into class and started the lessons— always, always, she forgot to take roll—while two of her students hid under her desk. They would have seen the entire class through from this perspective except that their delight in the prank, and their classmates' laughter, gave them away. Other missteps included her constantly confusing the names of two black girls—"Do we all look alike, Miss Mazur?" The problem was the girls did look alike.

She remembered other embarrassments. The class trip to the cheese factory where she stepped in something that stank up the bus. Those moments—all too many of them—when pride overrode discretion, and she let loose her voice in a communal song; she let her florid soprano flail upward and over the ordinary sound produced by those gathered at the start of the new school year. Her voice, a fat girl's vanity, drew too much attention in a school setting, and only in church could she freely sing. However had she managed to get through the first year at Siddons? Anna suspected it was finally her friend's good word, Sharon Feeney, the darling Miss F, who had known Anna at the university and had written on her behalf. The darling Miss F—"I can't carry a tune!"—was a favorite among the administrators. To be favored, a favorite, that was Anna's ambition, but she was not so confident of this happening as to decorate her apartment with the view of long-standing employment. This was her third year of teaching at Siddons.

Tim Weeks was thirty-three years old and had been at Siddons for six years. His apartment was darker and had no river view, but there was permanence in the oak shelves and books and photographs. Anna had no photographs; her personal history shamed her for being as ordinary as mud. Her mother had worked in a nursing home and her father on assembly at the GM plant. Their house was split-level in a ditched development, no water in sight, stunted trees, and culs-de-sac. Her father once in the car saying, "Oh lordy, Annie, it's just a fancy word for dead end."

Marlene

On clubs afternoons when Marlene was free—she wasn't a joiner—she walked to the hospital and sat with Astra Dell. If others were there or arrived, she cut the visit short and only left off whatever she had brought to read to her because Astra had said she loved being read to, so that is what Marlene did. She read stories from *Dog*

Fancy's "Therapy on Four Legs." She brought in stories about heroes and miracles that might make Astra feel good, and they did because she smiled when Marlene read them. Astra said, "Marlene, you're weird," but she smiled when she said this. Astra always thanked her, and she thanked Marlene in a genuine way. Her smile seemed to Marlene entirely sincere; even on those afternoons when she was in pain and noddy with medicine, when her voice broke and she only waved good-bye, Astra seemed glad to have seen Marlene, and so Marlene came to the hospital on other days, not just clubs afternoons. She would have visited on the weekends except the weekends were Mr. Dell's. On this day, as on so many days, Marlene Kovack left school and her last name—the nasal sound of it when said at school—she left behind, and she walked along the East River down the broad avenue to the hospital.

The spired entrance was marbled and churchlike in its serious human traffic, and Marlene was an old parishioner, a woman in black on her way to prayers. She didn't have to ask where, she knew. The back banks of elevators, the higher floor, the long corridor, turn left, and another five rooms down, and she was there, Astra's room, the door ajar and sometimes other visitors but most often not, most often on clubs afternoons it was only Marlene. Once when Miss Mazur and Mr. Weeks had come, Marlene had stayed on. She wanted to know teachers the way Astra knew teachers, and Marlene liked Mr. Weeks. Marlene did not know Miss Mazur, but it was her opinion—and she shared it later with Astra Dell—that Mr. Weeks felt sorry for Miss Mazur, which was why he was with her. Miss Mazur's face was wildly askew. Every feature went its own way, and her nose was a large distraction. Most clubs afternoons Marlene had Astra Dell to herself. Astra sometimes slept; she opened her eyes sometimes only just long enough to say, *I'm not feeling very well.* Astra wasn't feeling well on this clubs afternoon, so Marlene did not stay but left a note on the bedside table for her signed *love.* And for this, Marlene thought better of herself, and once home she was a sharpened arrow thrummed from the bow and hitting its target. Steadfast, selfless, purposed to comfort her friend, her only and her best. Couldn't she say that? Yes, Marlene thought, however unacknowledged, she was Astra's best friend.

A Daughter

The nurse informed them that Astra wasn't feeling very well today. "We won't stay long," Lisa said. Miss Wilkes in a louder voice to Astra, "We just wanted to say hello." Lisa moved away from Miss Wilkes so that Astra could see her and she could see Astra, but the sight of Astra weakly propped against the pillows surprised Lisa, who had not visited before and had had no idea of how worn away her friend would be, how see-through thin.

Lisa and Miss Wilkes, uncertain in the semi-dark of Astra's room, whispered to each other, was Astra asleep?

"I'm not asleep," Astra said.

"'How are you' seems like such a stupid thing to ask," Lisa said, "but how are you?" One stupid question after another followed. And afterward in the booth at the coffee shop, Lisa said she was stunned. Astra seemed to have shrunk already. Lisa said, "Obviously, I didn't know what to say."

Miss Wilkes was forgiving. She said she liked Greek coffee shops. Posters over every booth—white, hilly villages, crags to the sea. Behind the glass door in the refrigerated case the usual desserts, thickly frosted cakes, rice pudding, liquidy fruit.

Wet water glasses were swiftly set before them and then the heavy coffee-shop crockery, coffee for Miss Wilkes, hot water and a tea bag for Lisa, who sighed out how unfair it was, Astra Dell, how awful, how confusing, how messed up it was, and it was! No one ever said the world made sense, but Lisa had expected that hard work and earnest intentions would pay off to some degree. Maybe the school reward system was the problem. "We need a much more arbitrary system," Lisa said. "Grades should be picked from a hat." No more elections and auditions. The fateful nature of the world was what should be taught because outside of school that was how it was. Money, scarce among the teachers and rarely talked of and then as an evil, was undervalued in school when, in fact, it decided so much. Lisa said that Suki Morton would end up at Brown because of it.

"Who are the Mortons?" Miss Wilkes wanted to know.

"They're the soup people."

Miss Wilkes said, "I'm ignorant of high-end experience, so I don't feel the lack."

"I don't either," Lisa said, "at least not until the girls come back from spring vacation blonder and tan. Then I'm jealous." She shrewdly shoved aside her parents' summer home on the Jersey shore.

Miss Wilkes remembered a senior with high style whose disc player blew up in Dr. Meltzer's class. There were sparks, or that's what everyone said. Dr. Meltzer screamed at the girl, "Who do you think you are?" One of the drawbacks of the fourth floor: Dr. Meltzer was there, throwing chalk. "I hear him screaming a lot."

"Dr. *Belt*zer," Lisa said.

"So he said, 'Who do you think you are?' and she said, 'A Du Pont.'"

There were, in Lisa's opinion, so many ways to be disappointed in school. "Prize Day, if you want to know. Prize Day is a reason to give up. I lose sleep, friends, and hair, so I can sit through an eternity of the 'Every-thing Lisa can't do' show. I have to pay attention be-cause my mother will want to know names so she can torture me with them."

"But you've won prizes."

"The nice-girl prize, yes, twice. I had them fooled."

"You're not a nice girl?"

"No," Lisa said, pulling at the skin on her thumbs, "I'm not a nice girl."

"I have that habit, too."

Lisa said, "I know." She said, "Graduation seems so far away," and she sighed theatrically. Lisa said, "I don't really want to talk to anyone at school anymore. Not because of you. Just because there is no reason to make an effort. It's not real at Siddons." Margaret Schilling and Jennifer Mann, stupid, glossy, social girls, not long out of Siddons, were on the gossip shows now. Margaret Schilling had recently posed in an emerald dress with a pug in her arms for one of those horsey magazines. "My mother buys *Town and Country*." Lisa thought many of the girls in her class were simply making themselves into the perfect corporate wives of tomorrow. "I heard, swear to god, word for word, Alex Decrow say, 'All I want is to smoke and party and marry a rich guy.'" Lisa thought that the importance of money should be taught; at least then girls would be prepared and might go through life less bitter.

"Are you bitter?" Miss Wilkes asked.

"I'm growing more disappointed every day," Lisa said.

"And why is that?"

"I am sure Suki Morton does not have the grades or the numbers, but she will get into Brown. She's not very smart, but she has a lot, a lot of money. So there's one reason to be bummed."

"Any other?"

Lisa had to pause over this question. "Health. Health guarantees. I expect to stay healthy because I eat cautiously, and I exercise and I don't smoke—well, now and then I have a puff—but then I look at Astra Dell, who has led a pure existence, and she is sick." Lisa said, "She's been a vegetarian for three years!"

Miss Wilkes rose abruptly and said, "I'll be back." In the bathroom she ran cold water over her wrists. Her face in the mirror seemed to waver, and she did not want to go back to the booth. *Not because of you:* What had Lisa Van de Ven meant by that remark? They had been spending a part of every school day together, but this was the first time they had ever gone anywhere together outside of school. She did not want to open her mouth—too many teeth—but she did when she saw Lisa smiling at her return. Miss Wilkes had never perfected a closed-mouth kind of smile; besides, she was too big a woman for that. "We should get the check," Miss Wilkes said, and she gestured to the waiter.

"I'm all right," Miss Wilkes said. "Don't worry. Hospitals upset me."

"Yes."

"No," she said, and she put her hand over Lisa's to stop her from sliding over money. Her hand over Lisa's looked large, and she kept the girl's hand under. Was the girl embarrassed? The salt and pepper, the cup of sugars, the poster, the booth—what else was there to look at? She looked at her hand over Lisa's, and Lisa, she saw, looked at her, and the girl made no effort to turn away, and so this was how it demonstratively started, although Miss Wilkes was not sure she wanted it started. She should never have suggested they visit Astra together, should never have prolonged the afternoon. But here they were in the coffee shop without words—of course!—with a gesture, followed by another, a caressing thumb. Her large, chewed-up thumb over Lisa's smaller, chewed-up thumb. "You're wearing polish," Miss Wilkes said.

"My mother says it looks cheap."

"I don't know about that."

"It does," the girl said, "but I like it."

The salt and pepper, the poster again—what else was there to look at? Now Miss Wilkes was embarrassed or more embarrassed than when they had begun this, for this was a beginning for them. This was what happened at beginnings. Tentative, self-conscious, clumsy, clumsily affectionate starts. *I, I, I,* the stuttered confessions. She might say, *I'm not very good with words,* but Lisa was lifting her hand out from under, she was squeezing the older woman's hand, she was laughing a little and patting Miss Wilkes's hand, saying, "What big teeth you have, Grandma," saying, "Let's go, it's late, you can walk me home," saying, "Don't be disingenuous, Janet. You knew I was a take-charge person."

Miss Wilkes—Janet Wilkes—was at least ten years older than Lisa Van de Ven, but in this moment she felt as if she were the student.

Mothers

Car Forestal's name did not come up at the senior parents coffee, although Astra's did. A number of mothers could have told stories about girls from other schools, but only Mrs. Cohen recounted to the group what she had heard was happening at St. Catherine's and Norris-Willet. "The pipes are rusty from girls being sick." Several mothers bemoaned their helplessness. The college counselor said it wasn't happening at Siddons.

"*It*—what isn't happening?" Mrs. Van de Ven asked, and Mrs. Cohen explained the acidic effects of throwing up. Mrs. Cohen said, "You and I don't have to worry about that problem."

"What does that mean?" Mrs. Van de Ven asked.

Car Forestal was the unnamed girl Mrs. Van de Ven described as a latchkey kid. *Some latchkey* was what Mrs. Cohen thought. Latchkeys, more like it. The father had some three or four homes, didn't he? And just where was Mrs. Forestal now? Why wasn't she at the coffee?

"Poor little rich girl."

"Poor little poor girl."

"Precocious."

"Depressed."

"Unwell."

CHF

Car Forestal lay on her bed smoking, swishing her feet, and feeling with the toes of one the smooth, polished toes of the other. No classes until after lunch, and she never went to school for lunch; except for advisory meetings with Dr. D, she never even sat in the lunchroom. The oily-gravy odors made her sick.

Astra occurred to her and how weird it was that she, Car, who smoked and drank, was healthy while her best friend was sick. Good could be wrung from dwelling on Astra. Comparatives were meaningful.

Now Car was sad, and she thought she should call her father. Astra he would understand. She would call him if she knew where he was.

Marlene

Marlene let her red pen trail to the center of the lined page to draw circle over circle over circle, petal, petal, stem. One flower, two, in smears of them, second-period math class. The old crowding in of the big terms: free will or fate. Underneath the gobby flowers, she drew an enormous, ornamental, biblical *A*. Astra Dell's dying: What did it mean to them all in this overheated room? Check-plus, best girl, A, Astra, Astra Dell. Marlene Kovack wrote *Astra Dell* in her notebook; she wrote over and over the letters to the sick girl's name; she fattened each into a cartoon.

"Marlene?" Miss F scolded in questions. Death adrift, an odorless gas in the room, Marlene Kovack felt its woozy effects and was glad when the bell rang and she could leave off math and numbers.

Out of school, she felt prettier—Marlene sat out recess and her next two frees in her apartment in the bathroom some twelve blocks away, and here she thought about Astra Dell again and Astra Dell's father and Astra Dell's mother, who was dead. When Marlene was ten, the only mother with a face had been her own mother, Theta Kovack, even then droopy, beaked, a slot for a mouth, and thin hair fluttered to balding—an embarrassment. Marlene saw her mother as she was, and Marlene had seen Mrs. Dell as she was, too. Mrs. Dell had given school tours. Right up to her violent end,

Mrs. Dell was giving tours; she had stood just behind the visitors in the doorway to Miss Hodd's English class and smiled at her daughter. Marlene had seen Mrs. Dell's face—eyes, nose, mouth matched up in small perfection, very pretty. A softer Astra, orange hair not red. Why couldn't Mrs. Dell have been her mother? Traitorous thought.

One day Astra Dell's enormous hair clip snapped off (that's how heavy Astra's hair was), and Marlene had found the hair clip and kept it. The clip was tortoiseshell and greasy from Marlene's rubbing it. She rubbed it now and looked under the ledge of the bathroom sink, junked up with soap and dismal.

Siddons

Impossible in the face of impossible, implausible, some of them imminent, defining decisions on the way: early apps. Early applications.

"One thing you have to say about our class," the two Elizabeths said, "we don't talk college."

"I leave that to my mother," Lisa said.

None of the girls—save for Ufia, Saperstein, Song, and Elizabeth G., who were applying for early admission—wore college sweatshirts, but that didn't mean the rest of the class hadn't picked up shirts and caps from their own first-choice colleges and wore these souvenirs at home. Kitty Johnson hoped to go to Williams and wore purple scrunchies; Alex Decrow hoped to go to the Rhode Island School of Design; Suki Morton, Brown; Lisa Van de Ven, Brown; the other Elizabeth, Brown; Edie, Penn; Car, Harvard or Columbia—*I'm allowed to have two favorites;* and Astra? Where did Astra want to go to school?

Marlene Kovack said . . . didn't say really, mumbled.

Alex and Suki

"Bite me," Suki said.

"I know," Alex said, and they shoved closer together on the red block, smoking, and talked about Astra Dell, how the day after her mother's funeral, Astra Dell had come back to school, and that was typical of Astra, wasn't it? "She's perfect."

On this damp day, Alex and Suki saw so many mothers with and without babies passing the red block on their way to the expensive coffee shop with its seacoast cottage interior. There they all were, the young women in oversize barn coats and tight pants and narrow sling-backs they wore sockless. Such were the signs of ease. Wrist-size ankles, bones, bones, blushed faces, woodsy hair. Pedigreed dogs, rare breeds. See the chocolate Sussex spaniel in his puddled leash outside the store? "Woof to you!" Suki said to the midmorning mothers, and Suki wiggled—she always did this in passing—she flitted a little ass in her rolled-up uniform skirt on her way back to school, recess over. In the hallways the worn-away mothers were giving parent tours.

Siddons

Miss F, after lunch, on the elevator, kept herself aloof in the corner to avoid any sudden moves of the dangerous seniors stooped by the weighty, sharp weaponry of books they carried on their backs. "Watch, watch," Miss F said, making her way out. Four from the class of '97. They seemed happy enough though her own students protested their despair. Unhappiness weighs more, of course, not that Miss F had known it. Now this, this wonderful girl, Astra Dell, was sick. For the class of '97, the year would be marked by this event and its outcome. Pray heaven, the girl lives.

Alex and Suki

Alex Decrow bought a box of cards and left one on quick Quirk's desk: a duck with the message, "You quack me up." Alex had drawn a line through the word *Valentine* and written above in bold caps *QUIRK*.

"Alliteration. That ought to help your cause with our college counselor," Suki said.

"I just want to get it straight with her who I am and where I want to go to college."

Mothers

Mrs. Van de Ven, whenever she gave a school tour, knew at least some of what was happening on that day. "And a lot happens," she explained to the couple as they stood in the lunchroom. Middle-school soccer, council, upper-school morning meeting, JV volleyball vs. Norris-Willet, varsity volleyball vs. Norris-Willet, Diversity Book Club. The Dance Concert was already in the making, and ahead were the spring musical, Gilbert and Sullivan, and the class-eight play with the Alford boys. Mrs. Van de Ven gave the couple copies of the *Quill* and *Folio*, the middle- and upper-school literary magazines. "Award winning," she said. Other publications included the school newspaper, the *Siddons Observer*, and the yearbook. Lots of clubs, a Rainbow Coalition—gender issues, Mrs. Van de Ven said, dropping gender issues into the soup of the tour as with a slotted spoon, carefully. Gospel Choir, Knitting Club, Save Tibet. Community service obliged girls to work outside the school at soup kitchens, hospitals, nursing homes, schools. Sixty hours needed to graduate. Mrs. Van de Ven said that yes, hard to believe, this was her last year as a Siddons parent. "Next year I'm a past parent. It makes me kind of sad. I feel as if I'm graduating myself, and in a way, I am."

CHF

The skipped lunch entitled Car to a Tasti D-Lite, and it wasn't too cold for a Tasti D-Lite, but it also meant that after the cone she would have to run the reservoir. Dinner was never really a problem. Her mother usually said okay to most of what Car did. *Okay* from her mother with a hurt expression. Last night, the night before, any night with her mother was dangerous. The way they sat, each at her end—a centerpiece, a mound of acid greens and champagne grapes, antiqued hydrangeas as from another century, was pushed back a little. "The better to see," her mother said, and her expression at the other end of the table was skeptical or indifferent. Her mother sat erect with her wrists against the edge of the table, hands prayered, nails red. No plate at her mother's place. Her mother wasn't hungry. Oh, all this about her mother! Car had forgotten her mission, and she walked back up the street again, passing classmates carrying frothy coffees. With Astra sick, Car was on her own. This was what it would feel like in France with her father in the spring: tromping in oversize boots through rooms that echoed.

So another letter in her head started to Astra, another explanation, but then what? Talking, talking, talking about herself. Originality was hard to come by on Fifth Avenue, walking north, park side, under the dark overhang of trees in an odd and balmy patch of late October. Noon now, lunch now, and Car on a walk. What could she say to Astra in the moment that would not be wrong? How could she write to Astra about the clean out-of-doors and how rarely happy she was in it?

Fathers

As Dr. Byron had explained, Astra was still growing. The environment for the nasty cells was as nourishing as school. Dr. Byron had assured Mr. Dell that they could talk anytime. Where was Grace to take notes? Anaplastic high-grade fibrosarcoma, a rare connective tissue cancer: What was he to make of these words, he, a lawyer? "Fuck," he said, "Goddamned, mother fuck," and he went on cursing on the street. Mr. Dell was not a man to swear. He moved to hail a cab, then decided he would walk the forty blocks he had to home.

Unattached

Anna Mazur said the teachers' lounge smelled of the movies, and Tim Weeks agreed and asked did she want to take a walk? The day was blue; the trees were in a flap. Fall color, October.

"*Davidenja!*" Tim Weeks said to one of the cleaning women as he and Anna Mazur passed an open door along the hall on their way out. Then Tim Weeks was smiling and looking only at her again, saying, "That's the only expression I know. I think it means 'good night.'"

Tim Weeks smiled at her; nonetheless, Anna Mazur continued to talk about her brother. His cancer—also rare. "My mother put her hands on his face, and that was the beginning of the end," Anna Mazur said then, "Why am I talking like this on such a beautiful day?"

Siddons

Lisa stood to address them and said that Astra Dell was devoted to dance and was a senior and a survivor—Lisa was not—but that some of the other seniors in Dance Club, Kitty Johnson and Ufia Abiola, were survivors. They had known Astra from the beginning. Alex Decrow and Suki Morton were survivors, too, though they were outside at the red block, smoking. Edie Cohen, who came to Siddons in seventh grade, and Kitty and Ufia sat on the floor, arranging themselves into blown-out, solemn flowers, and sounded assent that something nicer than flowers should be sent. Something done but what?

"I've got some ideas," Lisa said.

I can't believe it: the chorus in the senior lounge, Dance Club members packing up for home. Some stories were told, and one in particular because it had happened to so many of them. Eighth grade, the Shakespeare play with the boys from Alford. Francesca Fratini was Helena—in heels, almost six feet tall, using Will Bliss as a shield—she was very funny, but Francesca was always funny.

Will Bliss was another story. Talk about conceit.

Will Bliss, eighth grade, even then a boy of lovely shape and wavy hair he wore behind his ears. Will Bliss! Preposterous name!

"Everyone had a crush on him!"

"Had?" Alex said. "Speak for yourself!"

Will Bliss and Astra Dell broke up because of Car.

"I don't understand that relationship," Lisa said.

"Astra is loyal."

"Have you seen her senior page?" from one of the Elizabeths.

"She did it already?"

"She said she's always known what she wanted to do," from the other Elizabeth.

"So what did she do?"

"She designed a page where she's looking over her shoulder at rows and rows of postage-stamp-size pictures of everyone she has ever loved. Miss Hodd and her cats and her horse and Car. A lot of teachers. Mr. Weeks."

"That hottie!"

"Gillian Warring wants to marry him."

"He knows how handsome he is."

How many times had Mr. Weeks been seen observing himself in the mirrors of evening windows? How many times seen making a face that he must have thought handsome?

Ufia, who rarely spoke unwisely, said, "Come to school in the dark and go home in it, and both ways take Madison Avenue—a person can't see the merchandise for her face."

Lisa said, "Once Astra told me the longest day of the year made her cry because every day after would be shorter."

"Don't even think it," from Ufia. "Astra Dell is not going to die. So stop crying!"

Girls were picking through the senior lounge and one of them was saying, "You think that's bad?"

"Suki," Alex said. "Did you hear me? I'm going to make this video for Astra. It's going to be funny."

"That'll be hard," Suki said.

"God!" Lisa said when Alex brushed past. "Air yourself out, girl."

The sound of Astra Dell's voice—impossible to call it up—but the inflection learned from her mother, her poor dead mother, that was the thing. Hearing Astra Dell hack around singing some twangy country girl's song, that was what Ufia said she missed, and the girls still in the lounge, all of them, agreed.

"I wish she were here."

A Daughter

"That's what I sent." Lisa's mother, calling from Sucre, was describing for her daughter a bouquet, mostly stargazer lilies, she had sent to Astra Dell. "Her father told me that Astra loved the stargazers."

"I would have done something," Lisa said.

"But you didn't."

"Oh, blank that."

"Watch it."

"I was going to do something."

"Oh."

"I hate you, Mother!"

"Astra Dell can have visitors at any time, you know."

"Whose friend is she, anyway?" Lisa said.

"I'll talk to you—" Mrs. Van de Ven began, but her daughter clicked off, mum on the visit she had made with Miss Wilkes to see Astra.

At the upper-school morning meeting, Miss Brigham had announced that Sarah Saperstein and Ny Song had been named National Merit Finalists; Ufia Abiola was honored by the National Achievement Program that recognizes black students; Karen Sanchez and Julia Alonzo were Scholars in the National Hispanic Recognition Program. Karen and Julia were among the top 2 percent of all students who self-identified as Hispanic on the PSAT. Lisa remembered the numbers and was pretty sure her mother had the news as well; her mother had been at school in the morning giving a parent tour. Her mother knew all about the top 2 percent, which explained her mother sending more flowers to Astra Dell—a sick girl was less a disappointment probably.

Fathers

Wendell Bliss (of the weak heart and well-known son Will) found a cheerful salad—red and yellow peppers cut in cubes like confetti—left by the housekeeper on the counter. There was a lukewarm chicken breast dressed up with parsley and little potatoes that he could reheat in the microwave if he knew where to find it. Stumped again by the serene expanse of stainless steel. Only the hooded restaurant stove with its prominent grillwork over the burners was apparent to him, but *Viking* was a word that came with men in horned helmets, and Wendell Bliss wouldn't think to touch the stove. He ate his lukewarm food; he ate slowly. After a while Marion Bliss phoned from Florida to check on what had been left him for dinner. He told her, and then he told her about Will and how he had said yes to an advance on the boy's allowance. He told his wife about Astra Dell, too, because he knew she would want to know. His wife knew so many people—they knew so many people—and one of her chief pleasures was rooting out what connected them. She was fond of saying, "Six degrees of separation!" The discovery of parallel experience and pattern was satisfying to his wife, but the unfairness in the allocations of suffering was something to ponder, that was a lozenge to suck on and so fall to sleep.

CHF

Car Forestal made art out of what was on her plate.

"It isn't fattening," her mother said, but Car said the sauce was tasteless, and she pooled it in potatoes, which she never ate. "You know I don't."

Mrs. Forestal said she didn't know why she bothered with a cook, and Car said she didn't know why either. Mrs. Forestal said she tried to please, and Car said don't. Mrs. Forestal asked Car was she this way in school, and Car said which way? Mrs. Forestal said don't bother, and Car said she wouldn't. Nothing she did was right, Mrs. Forestal said, and Car said no, nothing she, Car, did was right.

"I can't talk to you."

"I can't talk to you either."

"Every night this."

"I can't please you, Mother. Nothing pleases you."

"That's not true."

"You're always on my case."

"I am not."

"Listen to yourself sometime; you are."

"Don't be smart, Carlotta."

"I'm not being."

"You're excused, then."

"But I'm not finished."

"You are. You're only playing with your food."

"Okay, if you want me out . . ."

"Don't run off to your father's."

"I'm not."

"I know you."

"No, you don't."

"I'm warning you."

"Yeah, what are you going to do?"

"Don't leave this house . . . Carlotta."

"I'm going out for a walk. Can I go out for a walk, Mother? My best friend is very sick, okay? I need to be by myself for a while, okay? I need to get out of this place."

Siddons

Dembroski, checking off attendance in senior-class meeting, was calling out, "Decrow? Has anyone seen Alex Decrow?"

"After ninth grade no one ever makes perfect attendance," Kitty Johnson said to Car. "What happens to us all in tenth grade?"

In tenth grade Mrs. Dell was killed in an accident, not so uncommon in the city: An out-of-control car drives onto a sidewalk. In Mrs. Dell's case, a taxi driver had a stroke and drove onto the sidewalk, injuring three and killing one, Grace Dell. The news flared in the papers, a photograph, and then hissed out.

Grace Dell, Dies at 44; October 4, 1994. All those fours: four-four, four, four; four fours. "I bought into numerology for a while," Car said, then felt quick Quirk at the back of her neck wetly shushing: *shush.*

"I hope you know you're sitting at the Fat Table," Elizabeth F. said.

Greta Varislyvski seemed not to care or hear or even really see them but pulled her long self along the lunch bench until she was seated across from the two Elizabeths, Elizabeth F. and Elizabeth G.

Greta Varislyvski dully repeated, "Fat Table," as if she were answering the roll. Here was space to sit, and she had taken it. She was hungry. "I like to eat, too," she said. "All these girls counting calories. I'm not one of those."

The two Elizabeths were delighted then and told Greta she was welcome at the Fat Table anytime. The soy-cream sandwiches were under discussion. The Elizabeths knew that the soy-cream sandwiches they served in the cafeteria were disgusting, but they liked them, anyway. Elizabeth F. liked strawberry and Elizabeth G., raspberry cheesecake. Elizabeth G. insisted raspberry cheesecake was better. "It is, it is, it is," she said, and knocked against the other Elizabeth.

Greta Varislyvski made a face that might have been a laugh.

"Please," Elizabeth F. said, "don't yuck-yuck my yum-yum."

Suki and Alex

"Please," Suki said, "I'm eating."

"I'm glad *you* are. I don't know what this is."

"A Caesar salad?"

"Really?" and she held up a square piece of iceberg. "What's the good of being rich, if I'm going to end up eating at Two Guys! Suki, I will pay whatever it costs never to eat at Two Guys again."

"Wow."

"Look," Alex said, "I don't want to be with the hoi

polloi—that's the name of it, isn't it?" She said, "I know I am just a terrible snob, but honestly, Suki, why are we saving money? What's the point?"

"Something else is the matter, and I know what it is."

"Don't talk about him."

"I'm bored," Suki said. "Maybe after our salads, we should get our feet hennaed."

Siddons

The senior-class Halloween morning meeting was notable for the number of girls who came dressed as skinny icons: Car Forestal came as Audrey Hepburn, and Alex Decrow swagged around in short shorts as Dr. Holly Goodhead, with a fake knife and a conch. Suki, aka Twiggy, did up her enormous eyes and batted them at Dr. Meltzer, saying, "Can you guess who I am?"

"Death?" he tried.

Marlene Kovack was unusually ironic and came as Carrie in a blood-splattered prom queen's dress. Ufia, the black princess, wore a fruit headpiece and carried maracas but was obliged to explain herself as Carmen Miranda. "Doesn't anyone watch Turner Classics?" Edie Cohen and Kitty Johnson came as a couple, Raggedy Ann and Andy, and Sarah Saperstein and Ny Song, another senior couple, came as a Big Mac and french fries.

"Really sexy," Alex said to Ny.

The boom-box girls were singing along with Sheryl Crow, "If it makes you happy, it can't be that bad . . ."

Francesca Fratini was a "fun food" and came as a banana, and there were the usual number of witches, a policewoman with a riding crop, and a criminal in ball and chains, but the parade fell apart when a yodeling Heidi in a dirndl skated into the fun foods and knocked Fratini down. Lisa Van de Ven in a nurse's outfit with breasts as big as hams and padded hips came to the rescue, and Dr. D, in devil's horns and carrying a pitchfork, stood up to say, "Dismissed. To hell with you all!"

Fa La Lah

CHF

Car had tried to write it as a story, but it always came out an essay, a pushy essay full of complaint. "My father was using me to get his boyfriends" missed the real complications of Paris last spring. Walking arm in arm with her father through the lobby of Georges V had been fun. Was she mistress or daughter? He was purring corrections: "*poissons de* . . . not *poisons de*," and she was saying, "I am taking AP French, Dad. I ought to know."

Her father's frown was little; his skin was taut and cared for. "Oh, my daddy is a handsome man!" Fragrant and languorous, a man interested in pleasure, delights of all kinds. Museums and jazz. She could write this out, but it lacked what she saw when he walked away from her; she wasn't sure she could put it in words. She knew where he was in the dark recesses of a glassy bar, but she could not see his face. He came back eventually. On his own—he didn't need her—Car's father always fished up a beauty, a man, a man and a woman, a man and a woman and another man. He knew them from somewhere; he met them at the bar. Her father brought them all to the table, but Car was the one who entertained them, or so it seemed to her, answering questions about Siddons, talking Virgil and Sally Mann, Auden and Philip Larkin. Until it was late, midnight, a bit later, then her father took her back to the hotel and saw her to bed before he returned to the party.

Once at a café in an always dank, poor part of town, a yellow light over a table, a damp floor, once here, rushed to for shelter from the rain, breathless, cold, her father touched her. Her father was plucking her wet shirt away from her breasts. "Dad," she said. "Do you mind?" She was no mistress then; then she was his daughter.

"I'm sixteen," Car said to Madame de Ratignole at a cocktail party in honor of a well-known art critic. Car didn't know the art critic's name; she was in AP French lit. They were reading *Le Père Goriot*.

"Yes," said the hostess, who happened to be Dutch and knew six, seven, eight languages—something like that—enough to make Car feel embarrassed. *Bumptious* was a word she had learned from her father and should use to describe herself.

But was that party really such a good idea for a college essay?

Mothers

Surely Theta Kovack in the first week of November was the last parent to confer with the school's college adviser to decide on Marlene's college list. She sat in the cubby that passed for an office with its weary rah-rah wall of faded pennants; the office was humid—from crying? Theta sat in a saggy chair and scratched what she thought was a bite in the crook of her arm. The process, Mrs. Quirk was saying, was exciting. Think of every college applied to as a first choice. Marlene, who sat next to her mother, was pulling off the pills on her uniform skirt, and she did not look up when either woman spoke.

"Marlene," Theta said. "We're talking about you."

"Yes."

"Did you hear what Mrs. Quirk just said, then?"

"All the choices are first choices."

"So what are your firsts?" Mrs. Quirk asked.

Marlene, still worrying the skirt, said, "Wesleyan."

The adviser snorted. "A moon shot," she said. "What else?"

"Brown."

"Marlene, you and I have talked before," Mrs. Quirk said.

Theta was studying the map behind the adviser with the pushpins of where last year's class had landed.

The largest constellation of pushpins was in New England, but a lone pin in Florida and another in Arizona suggested there were other girls without the numbers who had landed somewhere.

"Think," Theta said to her daughter.

The two women looked at each other, and then they looked at Marlene, who was scratching her leg with the sharp heel of her shoe, making scratch marks wide as a ruler up and down her leg.

"Marlene," Theta said with angrier insistence, "you've had months to consider. What have you been doing?"

"I've been taking notes for Astra Dell. I've been visiting her and reading to her. What college is she applying to?" Marlene's expression when she looked at the college adviser was all chin.

The college adviser smiled. "That's not to the point, Marlene, and an expedient use of Astra Dell. What schools are you applying to, that's the question on the table."

This from "Quirky," the woman Marlene had described as always out of the office when a girl needed her. Quirky forgot a girl's name and where it was she hoped to be next September. Quirk was all numbers. Fifty, 75, 95 percent chances hyphened against the names of colleges on a final list she okayed. The witch wrote letters about every senior; she was the one to broker deals, and she had her favorites. Mrs. Quirk's favorites were sassy, scrappy, outspoken girls with no moon shots. Ufia, Darnell, Krystle, Karen, Teenie—she called them the Sisterhood; Mrs. Quirk was entirely confident of where the Sisterhood would land.

"I see you've got someone in Arizona," Theta said.

"The University of Arizona, yes, we have two girls there. You remember Mary Kate O'Neill, Marlene? She is very happy there."

"What about New York University?"

"What about it?"

Theta interrupted, "What about Wisconsin?"

"Now there you are," Mrs. Quirk said, with nods to Theta again and then eye to eye with Marlene. "You've a 75 percent chance of getting in, Marlene."

The Siddons School was all numbers, and Theta was adding them up. She was adding up six years of Siddons education. Here was math. Six years of her ex-husband saying, "Why not keep Marlene in public school? It was good enough for us." Six years of her own scramble. Loans and the interest on those loans. Theta was glad he wasn't here to hear what was good enough for Marlene. Marlene's choices were not the choices Theta had hoped—hoped perhaps unreasonably—to hear. If they had money, Marlene could afford to be a goof. But Theta was a receptionist at a dentist's office where retainers cost almost as much as she made in a month, and the privileged children with their crooked teeth kept losing them.

Oh! Last night's Chinese food was rising in Theta's throat; she would burp with her mouth shut and smile, but so many shames gusted in her: her cheap shoes, the floppy sack meant to pass for a purse, and other, more hurtful details—thin hair, no waist, tired hands. Middle class! She was ugly and average—not very smart. She reached over and covered Marlene's hand with hers. "We should look into Wisconsin." Theta said, "We should look into Syracuse. Daddy and I liked it there."

"Marlene should look," Mrs. Quirk corrected, and Theta felt slapped, and she burped.

Mrs. Forestal came into the head of school's office and saw that the school nurse and Car's English teacher, Miss Hodd, were also in attendance for this meeting that the head of school, Miss Brigham, had arranged.

"An emissary from the lower school was just here with news we have more rabbits," Miss Brigham said, and her expression, Mrs. Forestal noted, was kindly.

More puffy talk ensued.

Miss Brigham motioned they sit, which the three women did, in a circle around Miss Brigham's partner's desk. The desk was the only real antique in the room and had belonged to Miss Siddons herself. Miss Brigham now stood behind it. "We won't take up your time, Mrs. Forestal," Miss Brigham said. "We have some concerns about Carlotta."

"Thank you, Miss Brigham, for refraining from

using her nickname." Mrs. Forestal said to the nurse, "Her father thought it up and sadly it's stuck."

"Miss Hodd?" Miss Brigham asked Carlotta's English teacher to begin, and she did, with a lot of background—Car, *Folio*, the honor, Car as editor—but eventually got to the important part about a recent submission. Car's own work. "I told Car I felt obliged to show this story to the nurse, and she said she understood. She really didn't seem to mind, which made me wonder: Maybe this is a fiction, but I didn't want to take a chance." Now Miss Hodd gave a copy of the story to Mrs. Forestal.

"Does Carlotta see much of her father?" Miss Brigham asked.

"She hopes to see him over spring break."

"So she does see him?"

"She saw him last spring break."

"Dr. D says Car is worried about going to Paris," Miss Hodd said.

"Please, Carlotta is always worried about something."

The women made signs of agreement or understanding, of course; but the nurse asked, "Does she seem more anxious than usual?"

"There's Astra Dell, but frankly we don't much talk about Astra because there isn't much to say, is there?"

The nurse bowed her head, but when she looked up, she asked, "Carlotta has some eating issues, too, doesn't she?"

"I think so, yes."

The nurse said, "We think we should act before it gets more serious, Mrs. Forestal."

Mrs. Forestal spoke absently. "Yes," she said.

The nurse was more emphatic. "We think it is serious enough to warrant intervention."

"You think so?" Mrs. Forestal winced at the sound of her own voice, a high, stupid sound. Then she said again, "Yes," the gentle word, and she took up the sleeve of her sable coat and smelled it, which was to smell herself, her own sweet, perfumed, rich self. Then she could look up. Mrs. Forestal looked up at these women—the nurse, the English teacher, and the head of school—in wonder at their kindness. "I'm grateful you thought to call."

Miss Brigham said, "Of course. We love Car. There you go. I guess the nickname fits. We want the tomboy back."

"So do I." Mrs. Forestal began abruptly and only to Miss Brigham, saying, "I haven't read this story. My daughter doesn't share her work with me. She is a very neat girl at home. I don't go into her room."

"Of course."

"I understand," said the nurse.

Miss Brigham and Miss Hodd and the nurse, all three sat erect and ready. They wanted to work with Mrs. Forestal. They wanted to look out for Carlotta was

all. And with Mrs. Forestal's help, they believed they
could address whatever it was that was making it hard
for Carlotta to sleep at home.

"She is doing as well as ever. Her teachers give her
very good reports, but she often goes to the nurse with
headaches."

"She comes up to sleep in her frees."

Sleeping or not sleeping, apparently, was part of the
story.

Mrs. Forestal said, "I see Carlotta coming out of her
bedroom every morning." Her voice washed out as if
she weren't sure of this fact as she sat in a room, con-
spiratorially well-intentioned. "I've seen Carlotta eat
dinner." She sniffed at her coat sleeve again and recon-
sidered. "Well, maybe it's just playing with dinner. She
eats with her baby pusher and fork, I'm ashamed to say."

The nurse was making little sounds again.

"I'm thin," Mrs. Forestal said.

A generally uttered, quiet "Yes" from the nurse, the
English teacher, the head of school, then Mrs. Forestal
heard the rustle of her own slip against her wool suit,
heard the shush of her arms as she drew up her sable.
She was thankful to be rich. "Yes," she said, accepting
recommendations, some telephone numbers.

"Thank you," Mrs. Forestal said as she straightened
and looked at the story—her daughter's—in her hands.
The title was "Good Night."

Fathers

Mr. Dell did not understand what Dr. Byron had said except that it meant Astra would be off-limits to him; the radioactive rod to be sewn in her arm meant even to approach his daughter was dangerous. The nurses would attend to her masked. A rare cancer. Rare. Rare meant fatal, didn't it?

Mr. Dell missed his wife, and he resented the passing of time that took her further away from him. He wanted to look behind him and see her sitting on the edge of her chair but in no hurry to get up. Grace asking questions or telling little stories about her day. Walking tours, book clubs, social book clubs and church book clubs, Grace belonged, enrolled, was always a student. The way Grace laughed when she lifted off the pot lid and scared the cat with steam. "Serves you right!" Grace. To think of all the ways he missed her. The light adjustments she would make to his collar, his scarf, his tie, her hand's appraising caress as though she were attending to herself. The gift of this daughter, their only; after childless years, years of christenings and birthdays and the paper weight of someone else's child in his arms, the arrival of Astra did not surprise Grace. She simply took it as timely, a timely birth, but a birth she had nonetheless always expected. Her attitude was: We are graceful, handsome, philanthropic people of some small means, the Dells, and of course to us would come such a daughter.

Tomorrow that daughter would be off-limits. He could stand at Astra's door in a paper costume; he could look in; he could speak, but what could he say? Such suffering as hers could not be distracted except with drugs. Drugs on top of drugs. Wasn't his daughter too slight to withstand them? Morphine. Wouldn't it kill her?

Mr. Dell was a tall man with a kind face and little imagination, or so he looked to himself in the mirror of the window in his daughter's room. Most everyone he knew sometime got around to telling him that he was handsome, but he didn't see it. His eyebrows were too thick. And his interests? They were simple. He loved dogs and making breakfasts on Sundays. He rode horses. All of the Dells rode horses when they were on their farm in Virginia. They rode in Montana, too, and skied in Utah. Grace's legacy—a love of literature and decorative arts—was already in place in this girl of theirs. A lot of what he knew about art he knew from his wife; from his daughter he knew about modern dance. Last spring he had watched Astra alone onstage. He had seen her breastless dancer's body leap. She wore a tulle skirt in one dance, and in another she played in farmer's jeans. Whatever she wore, there was no way to hide her beauty. This was a fact he heard in the murmurs beside him. The point of her foot when extended, her ease and her arch and her surety, the prop of her red hair—a torch, a veil, a rag, a whip—contrastive accessories to the serenity of her wide-apart, beautiful face. By her bedside, befogged with so much feeling, unable to speak except to say good night, to pet what tomorrow he could not touch. He said, "Mommy is here," and then, because Grace would have liked it, they prayed, Astra and her father. He got up from his knees, a tall man, looking down at his daughter. "I'll be back in the morning," he said. "I can stand at the door. We'll sign to each other."

To see the girls moving broadly down the avenue laughing was to see girls in love, or that was what Wendell Bliss (father to the handsome Will) thought walking on the other side of Park with Marion's dog, Peanut. The girls looked familiar in their black short coats, black jeans, tottering boots. Where were they off to? Where were they all, the girls, all those girls Wendell Bliss had seen with his son at their apartment? Abundant hair and skinny feet. Where were they? And the girls he hadn't met who stayed at home on Saturdays. Were they baking cookies? That is what girls at home used to do, but this was New York. In New York a lot of girls found their way into his son's room. Marion Bliss asked that Will's door be kept open, but the door to his son's room was often shut. Home from boarding school, Will often squeaked past his parents' bedroom door in the predawn blue, and Will was not alone. Wendell Bliss never told his wife. He might tell her now if she were here or tell her how surprised he was to be old, but Marion was not here; she was still with her mother in Florida. She was in Florida and Will was on his way to Florida and he would follow without Peanut. ("Marion, the dog will upset your mother.") Marion's mother. This would surely be the last Thanksgiving in Palm Beach. Marion's mother had cancer. Cancer. Cancer everywhere you looked. Poor little girl, the one his son knew, the one in the play. There wasn't any question where that girl was tonight so close to Thanksgiving.

Marlene

Marlene Kovack was in Miss F's math class and going over the last test. Marlene had failed. Was she then a dummy? (Well, maybe in math.) But was she the dumbest in the dummy class? Was Marlene really a C student, or was she a C because of a ripe, damp quality she had? The pocket of skin beneath her eyes, a kind of blister, was discolored and sweaty as if the school air were tropical, and she, overheated from the exertion of changing classrooms and doodling in class. Marlene might not be a C if she were pretty and thin. She wouldn't be a C if she paid attention, surely, but Marlene stood up and walked out of Miss F's class—Marlene never asked permission but took advantage of her teacher's size and wore a certain malevolent expression she knew was a threat—and she dawdled in the hall. By the time Marlene returned, the problem was solved; the class was nearly over.

Now Marlene was lingering near the college office again, yawning in the face of yet another free and knocking around the hallway, showing herself to Mrs. Quirk. She asked the college counselor, "Mrs. Quirk, do you know who I am?"

Mrs. Quirk, a tall woman, tailored pants, pretended indignation. "Of course, I do," she said. "Aren't you . . ." and she laughed. "I'm kidding, Marlene."

Lisa Van de Ven went into Mrs. Quirk's office. Marlene had noticed Lisa was often stopping by Mrs. Quirk's office. Probably no teacher, Marlene thought, really knew who Lisa was, but Marlene did. She knew Lisa was not the nice girl she played at being with the teachers. *Does Marlene own a brush, or did she forget how to wash her hair?* Marlene remembered the Lisa Van de Ven of eighth grade, and that Lisa had not really changed.

Does she own a brush?

She always copies us.

Let's not be friends with her anymore.

She's overweight now. Sucks for her.
There's always one girl in your class that you hate.

Alex and Suki

"It's not as if we're the only ones," Suki said, but Mrs. Dembroski passed over this remark and wanted to know instead how Alex and Suki, both of whom lived within walking distance of the school, how they could be late for English, senior English, in this most important semester. An unexcused absence was a zero for the day in Mr. O'Brien's class, wasn't it? Didn't they know that?

"We know. We know, we know, we know. We're sorry. We're stressed. We can't keep up. Mr. O'Brien assigns so much. He expects us to remember everything."

"Okay. For now, it's just detention. Admissions needs help. After school on Friday, you can stuff envelopes."

The sound that whistled out of Alex as she left Mrs. Dembroski's office conveyed all her feelings, but did Dembroski really think stuffing envelopes was going to keep her from cutting O'Brien's first-period Monday class?

"I will never get into Brown," Suki said.

"You make me sick. There are practically buildings named after you there."

Siddons

Anna Mazur said, "Oh, to lose all that beautiful hair!" Anna's own sparse colorless hair sparked when she so much as touched it.

"Hair grows back," Miss Hodd said.

"Not that color," Anna Mazur said.

Miss Hodd said, "I let the nines write after morning meeting today. Nobody wanted to do grammar. Listen to what Camilla Berkey wrote: 'Helplessness scrubs us all clean of any hope we had of doing something, but the doctors are still dirty. They must not be touched with the sponge. No, they must not.'"

Mothers

Mr. Dell, who was not at the coffee, was mentioned by Mrs. Van de Ven as reading to his daughter. They had just started *Mansfield Park*.

And how did Mrs. Van de Ven know this? Mrs. Morton wondered.

"I asked," Mrs. Van de Ven replied.

The gathered fluttered and some of the mothers looked sad, but Mrs. Morton said, "That's Fanny Price, isn't it? It's a most unfortunate name." Mrs. Morton's deep, druggy, slow voice made several of the mothers laugh. The sound of Mrs. Morton was funny, as was the fact of how rich she was and well-read.

Mrs. Cohen took Mrs. Van de Ven aside and spoke softly, "Think of it this way: When Nanda Morton wakes up each morning, she has made more money than most of us will make in a year." Mrs. Cohen said, "And you know what that means, don't you?"

"I know what that means," Mrs. Van de Ven said. "It means Suki Morton is going to Brown."

"Oh please!" said loudly and in exasperation from another part of the room.

Theta Kovack had heard it all before and had juggled to come in late to work for this acidic coffee and reckless talk.

"Look at them, a class of forty girls," said Mrs. Quirk, the college adviser, "and all of them will find a college. The job is to make the right fit." Mrs. Quirk said it was important to encourage daughters to finish their essays before Christmas break!

Mrs. Saperstein and Mrs. Song wore wise, relieved expressions as their daughters had applied for early admission. These mothers didn't have to worry about essays anymore. "Thank god!" was what they said.

That poor Astra Dell. She was losing all that hair now, wasn't she? How, Theta Kovack wondered, had Astra Dell entered the conversation happening just behind her; but the girl had, thanks to Mrs. Van de Ven, who seemed absorbed by the subjects of Astra Dell and the girls making themselves sick at Norris-Willet.

CHF

Car pushed and smoothed and rearranged the food; she made patterns.

"Look, Carlotta, if you're not going to eat it—" Mrs. Forestal began, but all the air she had to argue with hissed out of her, and she sat quietly, seeming very small and vacant at the other end of the table.

Mothers

What were other people drinking over the Thanksgiving weekend? Miss Wilkes was drinking amber ale, and Lisa Van de Ven took a sip. ("I shouldn't but how else can I get inspired to write my essay?") Alex and Suki were drinking skim-milk lattes. Mrs. Van de Ven ordered pinot grigio for lunch with Mr. Dell. "He looks so thin!" she told her husband at the Post House for dinner. She explained that the doctor was willing to take a risk, "a combination of surgery, internal radiation, external radiation, a couple of chemo . . . ," but Mr. Van de Ven cut her off. They were eating, for heaven's sake, weren't they? "You may be," she said, "but I am drinking."

At the senior parents coffee, Mrs. Van de Ven said she was becoming an alcoholic!

The senior parents coffee had been very well attended. The college adviser, Mrs. Quirk, was at the coffee to answer any last questions about applications and what parents might expect for the next few months. Although the questions and advice seemed much the same as those of two weeks before, the mothers attended to what sounded rewound and repeated. Car Forestal's name did not come up. (It never did!) A number of mothers could have told stories about Carlotta Forestal or about other girls from different schools, but only Mrs. Cohen recounted to the group whatever horror she had heard was happening at St. Catherine's and Norris-Willet, and again several mothers bemoaned their helplessness.

A Daughter

Lisa Van de Ven sat in the kitchen in the best chair. "What the hell is this?"

"I don't know," her mother said. "Leave it if you want. I don't care."

"Oh, Mother."

"'Oh, Mother' what?"

"I know what you're thinking."

"Do you?"

"I do."

"I wonder."

Unattached

Anna Mazur came to the disappointed part of the Tim Weeks story and said, "I'm not pretty, Mother."

Her mother was silent on the phone.

"We're more like brother and sister than anything else." Anna sighed and asked her mother, "What do you think?"

Her mother thought that only baked or handmade gifts should be exchanged between staff and students at Christmas.

Anna said, "That's the rule, but people break it all the time."

"That's right," her mother said. "You got that ugly scarf last year."

"Yes, Mother. That ugly scarf from Hermès."

"It had stirrups all over it."

Anna said, "I don't know what to think about Tim."

"I'll tell you what," her mother said. "Don't think about him."

Siddons

The news on December 15 was bad—Astra still off-limits; and good—early admits to Harvard, Princeton, Stanford, and Trinity, all confirmed. Four girls were in college! School was over for them.

Kitty Johnson, who was waiting to confer with Mrs. Quirk about colleges, said to Car, "If you thought Sarah Saperstein was insufferable before Harvard, imagine what she'll be like now."

"Ny Song, too."

Kitty lowered her voice to confide in Car the decision she had made to avoid her adviser's elective. "I'm not taking O'Brien's course."

"Good idea."

"I'm taking Hodd's Families in Distress," Kitty said.

Miss Hodd, in another classroom, slid her battered *Warriner's* to the corner of her desk and launched herself into the middle of the classroom in her castered chair, one leg up on the seat, chin on her knee, all the better to listen to how the seniors in her English class felt about the news that Astra Dell was sicker.

"A whole group of crying juniors passed me in the hall. They didn't even look like the kind of people who would be her friends."

"They weren't Astra Dell's friends."

"A lot of people aren't really crying for her; they're putting on an act."

Marlene

Marlene's head was at a whistling boil when she waved good-bye from behind the window to Astra's room— and Marlene was wearing paper shoes, cap, and gown—so what did the nurses wear? she wondered. Someone had to go into that room. Marlene waved good-bye, mouthed, "Merry Christmas," then shuffled away in those paper shoes, relieved to be well and leaving the sleepy, balding creature in a pom-pom hat Kitty Johnson had knit the sick girl when it went out at school that Astra was losing her hair. First lines to college essays occurred to Marlene: "Walking along the hospital corridor to see my sick friend was an unsettling experience." Possible, but there was her dad essay, the one she had started: "My father looked me in the eyes and asked, 'Are you ready?' 'No,' I replied, and he pushed me overboard, and I sank deeper and deeper into a cold, enchanted realm." Her father had pushed her into China Lakes, but Marlene had always wanted to go scuba diving, and who was to say she had not?

Siddons

Five of the graduates from the class of '96, home from college, came to see the last day of school and the Christmas spectacle when 536 girls from grades k through twelve gathered in the auditorium, the seats retracted for the occasion, and in the middle of the room, the fake Christmas tree with its paper-chain decoration. The fifth, sixth, and seventh graders gathered in the balcony with their teachers while the other grades filed in: big sisters and little sisters, starting with the seniors and their kindergarten charges, hand in hand, an endless coil of girls wearing red and green accessories, candy-cane tights, and tinsel in their hair—"I'm one big present, just for you!" Gillian Warring mouthed to Mr. Weeks in the balcony. Around and around, the elevens with the first grade, the tens with the second, on and on, the students came while most of their teachers sat on the stage of the auditorium. A few of the old favorite Christmas and Hanukkah songs to begin—"You would surely say it glows, like a lightbulb!"—and then Miss Brigham in a Santa's hat, front and center on the stage, read from *The Polar Express*. Then some more songs until everyone's favorite moment: "The Twelve Days of Christmas," when the first grade began, "On the first day of Christmas, my true love gave to me," and the kindergarten girls, no bigger than feathers, were held up by their senior sisters to squeak, "Fa la lah." The dreaded moment, of course, was "Five golden rings," when the fifth-grade girls leaned over the balcony with their wagging hands outstretched and shrilly pitched the song. The sixth and seventh graders tried to outshout each other, and the teachers, predictably, frowned, but "Five golden rings!" always put the song on high, and there it stayed with some slight mumbled diminishment in the upper grades as the ninth grade mimed nine maids a-milking until, the moment anticipated, and the seniors stood, some of them already crying, and began their own Christmas medley—playful digs at teachers and Quirk, of course, and college horrors. The girls were often off tune and uncertain of the lyrics so recently composed. "Jingle bell, jingle bell, jingle bell rock, you might just think our essay's a crock . . ."

January

CHF

What could she write to Astra in the moment that would not be wrong?

> *Dear A,*
> *Maybe you feel like it has been a waste to have spent your life practicing for what turns out to be nothing. But you are lucky in some ways because you will know what it is like to die, and the rest of us will spend our lives wondering. I know that this isn't comforting at all, but I'm sure you'll be getting enough of that from others, and soon it will stop meaning anything. So I want to talk to you about your dying. I know you have envisioned your own funeral before. People missing you. People make the most impact on the lives of others by being absent.*

Car had faltered over other letters, but this one she sent.

Siddons

Mr. O'Brien was wearing his Irish pants, the thick Donegal tweed number that Suki and Alex always said must have made him sweat in manly places. In the over-heated classrooms, Mr. O'Brien was wearing these pants, and his shirtsleeves were rolled up.

"Oh," Suki whispered, "he is so hirsute."

"You know the ugliest words, Suki."

Mr. O'Brien was reading aloud again, "'I felt a Funeral, in my Brain, / and Mourners to and fro . . .'" He was leaning over his desk in his scratchy-looking pants and plaid shirt and talking about the speaker's point of view, asking his students if they had contrived an afterlife or heaven for themselves. "What does Emily Dickinson seem to be proposing here? The floating *then*, the narrative word, at the end, by itself, in the poem with lead boots and space, what does that lonely term suggest?" And he repeated the lines, "'And then a Plank in Reason, broke, / And I dropped down, and down— / And hit a World, at every plunge, / And Finished knowing— then—'" and he said again, "'then.'" Mr. O'Brien was asking the seniors in English, section Z, what was Emily Dickinson saying about the prospect of heaven? Kitty Johnson was taking notes, sensing her own funereal headache was on the way, not quite looking at Mr. O'Brien, but listening to Ufia hold forth on how scary the poem was because there was no satisfaction for the dead. No eulogy overheard, only scraping chairs and shoes.

Alex whispered to Suki, "I got up at seven to make this class only to be informed there is no fucking heaven." Alex was circling a circle in the center of her notebook, a vacancy, a black hole that grew larger as she spoke. "I mean, this is swell. Nothing to look forward to. I should have guessed."

Nothingness again, that odorless gas again; Marlene, in the back row, felt sick. She wasn't reading this poem with Astra. This poem would be an assignment Astra could do with someone else. Let someone else, let Car explain it, for Astra would insist—did insist, asked for whatever was said and done in class—because she planned to graduate with her class. "My minister visits. He keeps my spirits up," so Astra had said to Marlene, and who was she to suggest a darker outcome?

CHF

Dear Astra,
Maybe I am being morbid, but I'm not going to lie.
So you won't go to college or have a family, but
wouldn't you get tired of that? There are songs
about people like you, making you heroic just because
you're young but near the end. You can't stop this.

All you can do is pretend to be sad that you are leaving and smoke your medicine and hide your skill as if you are ashamed, but I know that you are happy this way. The only thing you have to excel at now is leaving, because you only get to once.

Another letter Car suspected she should keep in her drawer, but she didn't.

"Carlotta, are you going to eat that or not?"

"I'm cutting it, aren't I?"

"Have you talked to your father about spring vacation?"

"I don't know why you ask me these things when you already know the answer, Mother."

"Why would I know the answer?"

Mrs. Forestal crossed her arms and caressed herself and was soothed by how thin she was. St. John Knits were made for thin women; their close-fitting jackets showed off long arms. Car had the same long arms, although her mouth suggested she could be a larger woman. Was it any wonder then her daughter would cut and cut and cut her meat until not much of it seemed left?

"Don't bother," she said as if speaking to herself.

"'Don't bother' what, Mother? What are you talking about?"

"I'm going to St. Bart's, and you're welcome to join me."

"Thanks."

"We can eat mangoes and sit in the sun and read and swim." All the time she was talking, Mrs. Forestal felt of her arms, put her face against her arms and smelled—Norell was still a wonderful fragrance, wasn't it?—and she felt slightly comforted. She liked her wrists, too, and the prominence of the bone and the color of her skin.

"When are you going out tonight?" Car asked.

"It's an eight o'clock curtain," Mrs. Forestal said.

"And you're seeing?"

"I don't know. Your grandmother bought the tickets.

"Do you like this color?" Mrs. Forestal asked. She meant her St. John Knit. "Is it too much like one of Nana's colors?"

Suki and Alex

A tooth just simply fell out. Cracked, fell out. One of the big grown-up teeth, a fat one in the back, gone—like that.

"Oh my god," said Suki, who did and did not like to hear terrible news, but this kind of next-to-death terrible news about Astra was really, really, really horrible.

"I think she is . . . ," said Alex.

"If she does . . ."

Alex and Suki, pre-exams. Stressed, really stressed now, but at least it was snowing, and they were walking past Will Bliss's apartment, the Bliss they seemed destined never to see, Will Bliss who had surely not missed any holiday, who was spending this one in Alta. Alta?

"One of those places."

"Why don't I ever know these things?" Alex asked.

CHF

Car Forestal called Astra from her father's apartment on the kitchen phone. She had been making a mess in the kitchen for a couple of days. A shallow sushi container, Starbucks cups, Starbucks napkins, biscotti. "I'm having a meltdown," she said. "I'm eating cookies. I'm ordering anything Annie's or Patrick's has to deliver. No one knows I'm living here. The staff's got off. Mom and Nana are in Bermuda. Mom thinks I'm at home with Arlette, and Daddy thinks I'm with whomever, and you know Arlette. She loves me; she would never tell Mother on me—besides, she thinks I'm visiting you most of the time. That's what I tell her, and I would come, Astra. I'd come to the hospital except you're still off-limits, aren't you?"

"Why are you talking so fast?"

"Starbucks, I don't know."

"I haven't been off-limits since Christmas. Marlene comes a lot."

"You can tell I don't see anybody," Car said. "I have *Folio* and that's it. Since when did you and Marlene become friends?"

"I was never not her friend."

"You never socialized with her."

"She keeps me up-to-date and reads goofy animal stories. Nothing sad. Not like your letters, thanks."

"Astra."

"It's good. You keep a person on her toes, Car."

"I can't bullshit you, A."

"No, keep the letters coming. Marlene likes them."

"Marlene."

"She means well. My little friend Teddy from across the hall sometimes comes over to hear Marlene read to me. She brings me my homework. I help her with math."

"Could you help me with mine?"

The sad part for Astra was that she didn't always know Marlene was in the room. The nurses had to tell her it happened. "I'm so often asleep. Watch. Later I'll forget we even had this talk."

Car said, "Oh, why do you have to be sick?" She mushed wasabi into soy sauce with her finger. "I know it's trivial in comparison, but I really, really, really need to get permanently away from my mother."

"That's what happened?"

"Of course, that's what happened."

"What this time?"

Car told a mother-daughter story she had told before. This time sweaters, purses, pushers, spoons, but as before, there wasn't much drama in it. The setting was entirely indoors. "My christening spoon—Jesus—what do you make of that?"

The clock on the wall chimed four while Car's watch read something else.

Time for Astra's visitors. She got them almost every afternoon and who would you expect? "You'll never guess," Astra said. "No. It's not. It's Mr. Weeks. Miss Mazur is here, too."

Unattached

Tim Weeks thought what was happening to Astra Dell was private. What business did he have in her hospital room? He didn't talk very much; instead he looked out the window at the river. He remarked on the view, then the current's roil, and the oily-colored scarring on her arms reminded him of what he had heard about rods and radioactivity, but he did not ask Astra what had happened. Tim Weeks asked nothing but looked around the room and out the window again at the river and the bridges and the islands beyond the bridges.

Astra was saying that when she saw the little children who were sick, then she really felt sad. Hearing this, Tim Weeks had to look at her again, and what he saw made him sad, for what was Astra Dell but a child, a child who had learned no other way to behave than gallantly, a child whose benevolent spirit seemed to swell even as she steadily grew smaller. To look at the sharp knobs of her shoulder bones, her wrist bones, her flimsy bones was to look at mortality, the grotesquely insubstantial self. The netting of blue under her throat and along and up her jaw was visible and seemed to pulse when Astra spoke, and she didn't speak a lot but she got thirsty. She drifted off.

"Sorry," she said.

"Why should you be sorry?"

"I'm making friends here. Next time I'll introduce you."

"We've overstayed."

"Oh, no. I'm so glad you came. I miss school. I miss my teachers."

"We'll come again."

Mr. Weeks smiled, but once outside he said, "I think I shouldn't see her this way."

But when Tim Weeks spoke about Astra, his voice didn't sound woeful but romantic; moreover, Anna Mazur could see why the woman walking toward them on long legs would distract him, but to shove into life so soon after visiting a sick girl on a blasphemous ward was unattractive even in this most attractive man.

The perverse part was that in that moment Anna loved him.

They shared a taxi home from the hospital, although Anna insisted she get off at Eighty-second and Third so that Tim Weeks could cross at Eighty-sixth. She didn't need a door-to-door escort.

"Do you get the picture?" Anna, on the phone to her mother, was relating the afternoon visit to Astra Dell with Tim Weeks.

"He is vain, but who wouldn't be with a face like his?" Anna had already told her mother that she liked him, that she liked Tim Weeks a lot, but what had started in October was the same in its intensity in January. Then Anna told her mother about the moment on the street when the pretty girl had passed them. How all of his attention was taken up by this approaching woman and his ambition to win her heart. What did this say about Tim Weeks?

Her mother asked, "Do you do anything else besides visit the sick girl?"

CHF

Off the phone, Car sock-slid around the kitchen island and out the door into the hallway, past the dining room, the living room, the library, veering to the carpeted hall that leafed into walk-in closets and the central bloom of Daddy's bedroom.

Car did not look into the bedroom but turned around and kicked up the carpet and slid on the hallway floor back to the kitchen, around the island, over the icy marble, out. She repeated this tour of the apartment until the kitchen clock chimed six, although her watch read six thirty. She was out of breath, but she took up the phone again, and when Astra answered, Car said, "I'm too fucked up to visit. I hope you know that."

Siddons

The learning specialist was there to help girls in the upper school, especially ninth-grade girls, organize themselves for exams, although even she admitted many of the girls already had good habits. Many had a plan. Double sessions with tutors, stockpiled Post-its, organized notebooks. Some rented the movie for the first time (or again); some bought the book on tape. *CliffsNotes* were shared, although they had been pronounced as nutritious as bread someone else has chewed and spit out. In fact, *CliffsNotes* really weren't read much. Most girls arduously reread. Their books glowed in the dark with pink and yellow marked passages. Some books seemed entirely painted. Fat with use and notes and flagged with Post-its, the books were as homely as gummed toys.

"I'm contemplating dropping out," overheard in a *Folio* meeting, Car Forestal presiding.

"Don't worry. A B here translates into an A anywhere else. The colleges know this."

"Phew," Suki said to this news. "Like I'm really relieved."

CHF

"Nobody wakes up in the morning trying to burn. Believe me, Dad, that's not my ambition."

A Daughter

Lisa had never been to Queens before, but she asked directions and found the street and proceeded through the door, up the elevator, and down the hall toward an escalating smell of onion. She knocked at the door and opened herself to Miss Wilkes's embrace, to the fuzzy, unwashed, brown disarray of Miss Wilkes in her oniony apartment. Miss Wilkes—Janet—cleared a space and then she hovered. "I haven't had company since Marie," she said. "Just Taffy," and Janet pointed to a large caramel-colored mound of fur making little *m*'s of sound, whiskers twitching.

"I'm allergic."

Janet moved between Lisa and the cat. "Oh dear, this whole place is cat!"

"It's only if I get close."

"Oh god," Janet said, and she brushed at her own clothes, but the caramel flecks of Taffy adhered. They could go somewhere else, but they had come to want privacy and for the first time had it. Lisa took Janet's hand and let herself be led into a back bedroom where one of the windows fronted brick. The buildings were close; the view was scary. The lumpish bed was covered in something coarse and maroon colored that Janet threw aside. "Scootch under," Janet said. Under the blanket then, under the cold sheet, against the warm, white shape, which did not smell like the usual Janet but a powdery, unexpected softness.

The truth was everything that happened did not feel good, although Lisa said she was only cold. It was cold outside. It was January. "But go on," Lisa said, and she let herself be held. She held still and said to the woman holding her, "Go on," even though some of what they were doing Lisa was shy of. "I think I may only be experimenting, Miss Wilkes," Lisa said, and the sound of the teacher title, *Miss Wilkes*, had the intended effect, turned the bedroom inside out, and they were both in school again, Lisa as the student.

"Yes," Janet said. "I understand," and after a while, "This is probably not something we should continue."

"Do you mean that?"

"I do."

This, this, no one else was doing this, *this* what Lisa was doing, which was experimenting, living, getting ready for college, ugly as it was in the ways it involved another's body.

"I don't think I've ever loved anyone," Lisa said. "Isn't that shocking?"

CHF

Miss Hodd said "Bedtime Story" was one of Car's best poems, and Car sent it to Astra because Astra would know what it was about.

A Daughter

Lisa Van de Ven e-mailed Josh that she had done it and discovered this kind of love was not what she was after. Josh was the only one of her friends to know what she was up to because, as she had told him, "to tell this tale would serve as an opportunity for some people I know to belittle and ridicule me, and I am the one who does this to others."

Mothers

Mrs. Van de Ven volunteered without anyone's asking. She had found the most reputable wig shop and taken Mr. Dell there, saying that one good feature was the range of styles they offered. Colors, yes, too, although nothing to match Astra Dell's red hair; her hair was not to be found in a shop. Carroty colors, moon yellows, silvers, whites in a schoolgirl style—long, straight, and banged—were available, and Mrs. Van de Ven held up the most orange model and asked Mr. Dell what he thought.

"Are you kidding?"

He thought he should buy his daughter earrings. Why try to hide the badge of her illness? The startled blue of her lashless eyes, the shadows of eyebrows—bald, bony, easily crushed—why bother with disguise or risk the horror of seeing her in a shifting wig, except that Mrs. Van de Ven seemed to think Astra might feel better about herself and her appearance in the "Cindy" wig. She held out the dummy head for him to touch the hair.

"See how lifelike?"

Mrs. Van de Ven didn't think he should pay for the more expensive human hair; the synthetic felt real, and, besides, the wig was temporary. "If you touched her scalp, I'm sure you'd feel stubble already."

Not stubble. He would feel the plates of bone. "I can't do this right now, Lettie."

"David."

"I've seen the wigs. I have to think about it. I have to speak to Astra."

"Then I'll buy it for her, David."

"Lettie, please."

Mrs. Van de Ven moved toward the counter with the "Cindy" wig, explaining to the saleswoman that this was the wig she wanted. At the same time, Mr. Dell held out his credit card. He said to the saleswoman, "I'm paying for this, please."

"David."

"I can't let you."

"And why ever not?"

He addressed the saleswoman, saying, "I'm paying," and the saleswoman looked at him and then at Mrs. Van de Ven, and when Mr. Dell held out his card, the saleswoman accepted it despite Mrs. Van de Ven's saying, "No, no, no. This is my treat. I'm the one who's insisting you get it. Give Astra a choice." She repeated this protest while the mechanics of the transaction went on between Mr. Dell and the saleswoman.

"Just sign here, please."

Mr. Dell also signed for the lunch that followed with Mrs. Van de Ven.

CHF

She told Astra the latest. "Now that Dad has a serious boyfriend, he doesn't need me to pimp for him, which is why, I'm sure, he's discouraging me from coming to Paris. He says I shouldn't. He says he's heard about my health. I bet he's heard. Didn't send him rushing home for Christmas, though, did it? I don't think I am going to go to Paris. I don't want to go."

Astra said, "Sometimes you do sound like the girl who uses her pusher too much, know what I mean?"

"Look, I know I'm being a brat, but I'm a seventeen-year-old American girl, Astra. I'm allowed."

Marlene

Was it as late as it looked outside?

Astra opened her eyes and said, "Time in here," but she didn't finish before she shut her eyes again. "I want a warm bath," Astra said. "The medicine makes me cold."

"I'm sorry," Marlene said. She was hurrying now, forcing folders into her book bag. Astra's otherworld voice scared her. She put on her coat and was almost at the door when Astra opened her eyes.

"It's too exhausting," Astra said, and she seemed to see dimly. "I can't be personal all the time."

Siddons

Dr. Meltzer repeated the question just asked him, "Can I give you the format to the exam? Do you really think knowing the format helps?"

How many times did Miss Mazur have to say it, "Yes, you should know the part of speech. Okay, okay. If you can use the word correctly in a sentence, I'll give you half credit."

"Extra credit? I never give extra credit."

"Will there be multiple choice?" The girls asked, "Maybe?"

"Can we not have an essay question?"

"I hate essays."

"I can't write essays."

"I never do well on exams."

"Even if I study for hours, I fail."

"I always fail."

"What if you can't read my handwriting?"

"Canweplease,pleasewriteinpencil?"

Alex and Suki

They were looking for Will Bliss again. They put on their lightweight coats despite the weather. They gave up on matching gloves but found good hats. They were taking long steps up Park Avenue, midnight by the clock, Alex and Suki, walking into the wind with their tiny coats wide open. Tube skirts, boots, candy striped, goofy hats with pom-poms. The snow, another snow, another storm predicted, had begun to fall. The big flakes seemed to be swinging in their descent, seemed to splash they were so large, and the ticklish pelt of them made the girls laugh, and it was hard to see for all the snow caught and melting on their eyelashes, watery drops on their cheeks, tears. They had given up on chemistry and Dr. Meltzer. Blue books, pencils, boxes of Kleenex.

CHF

A—
I've fixed this. I think it's better. I think you'll
understand it now. Please do. Not everything can be
funny.
I'm not even bothering to study.
kisses,
C

Mothers

Mrs. Forestal told the school nurse that she was doing everything she could to get Carlotta help. Carlotta had a nutritionist and a psychiatrist. "We have a cook. I sit at the table with her as often as I can, but I can't watch her every meal."

"Yes," the nurse said. "That's the hard part."

"Yes," Mrs. Forestal said. Why should she understand what the nurse was saying when she couldn't make sense of her daughter? The most recent poem she had been given to read didn't make any sense to her. So her daughter didn't like her body? Fine. Who did?

She reread her daughter's poem: ". . . and covering my eyes with tea bags, listened to the menagerie of bears, pigs, puff-white lambs, and crumpled tissues swarming the sheets." What was this all about? And why would anyone in her right mind admit to a "zoo-ish fragrance"? It made her think of apes. Was Carlotta trashing her father's place again? *Now at least it looks as if somebody lives here:* Carlotta's defense. Mrs. Forestal felt helpless and a little bored with Carlotta's bullish enthusiasms and clumsy lows. Maybe after exams.

Siddons

The snow that had fallen on Sunday was added to again on Wednesday, but by then Marlene Kovack had taken the math exam.

Miss F defended Marlene's grade, saying, "Marlene

must have studied. She sees Astra Dell, and Astra could have helped her with discrete math."

Poor Astra Dell was the general feeling. The girl would have been in AP calculus if she weren't sick. "I mean, she's in it," said Dr. D. "She just won't take the exam, I guess."

Exams were over in a sentence and returned just as fast.

Romance

Marlene

Marlene looked into Astra's letter basket and saw Car Forestal's hand, and she read the note because Astra was out of the room on some test. Marlene read:

> *A—*
> *I've fixed this. I think it's better. I think you'll*
> *understand it now. Please do. Not everything can*
> *be funny.*
> *I'm not even bothering to study.*
> *kisses,*
> *C*

Marlene was still in Astra's room, so she took up Car's latest letter, and she put it in her pocket. A note on a note card: It wouldn't be missed. Would it, would it, would it?

Sometimes when Astra turned the white radiance of her attention onto Marlene, when Marlene saw Astra considering her openly and clearly and fairly, then

Marlene knew what it was about Astra Dell that made her feel possessive of the sick girl. Marlene wanted Astra to herself and resented even the intrusion of Astra's father, although she was polite enough when she saw him.

"Hello, Mr. Dell. Astra's a little sleepy today."

A Daughter

Lisa told Josh (he had asked was she gay or not) that she was only experimenting with Janet Wilkes and Queens and all of it. "It turned me on for a while, but my mother ruined it. What happened was I'd be with Janet somewhere and I'd think I'd see my mother."

Siddons

"What's in the bag, Mr. Weeks?"

"A present for your girlfriend?"

"Try a bag of tests." Whenever he spoke, Mr. Weeks smiled or seemed to smile or was just about to smile, and the little girls and big girls, girls of all sizes, loud and silly, guileless and gentle, smiled back. The youngest faces were clean as how they came; the older were subject to hormones. Oh, hormones! That klieglight word they knew; hormones meant adolescence and suffering. "My hormones, Mr. Weeks!" Girls were bleeding all over the place, or that was how it sometimes seemed to him.

"Why are you crying?" one girl to another. "What did I say?"

"Why are you crying?" another to another.

"Why?"

"We didn't know you were coming."

"I tried to save you a place."

"She couldn't invite you; she could only have six friends."

"My parents are going to kill me."

"My grandmother is really sick."

The hallway's backdrop of posters: roundly muscled, oily heroines on the GAA board, drawings of the family—*ma mère, mon père*—from French V class. In-school polls and graphs for math. Popular after-school activities: Look at the pie and see what the middle schoolers do after school.

"Mr. Weeks? Do we really have to have a test on the explorers?"

"We do the explorers every year, Mr. Weeks."

"Why can't we just have a discussion?"

"You're so unfair!" said smiling.

"Why aren't you married, Mr. Weeks?"

"Do you have someone in mind?" he asked.

Unattached

Tim Weeks said his best and favorite year in school had been sixth grade, and he still felt like a sixth grader, which went some way in explaining his delight in the company of sixth-grade girls of all sizes: middle school, a mishmashed time, fifth, sixth, seventh, and eighth grades, class by class, grossly uneven rows of dangerous bodies, bodies in motion, sharply angled, full of feelings, bawdy, brazen children asking anything. "Was that your girlfriend?"—pointing to someone pretty when they had surrounded Tim Weeks on the street outside of school. In some ways, he was always in school. "We knew it was you on the street, Mr. Weeks."

"It was your walk."

"Sexy," from someone in the back, in a small voice but heard.

"What's in the bag, Mr. Weeks?"

"Is it something for us?"

"Yes." *Yes, yes, yes, yes,* from many sides, and each girl laughing and jouncing closer. Mr. Weeks, ringed by girls, girls jamming sidewalk traffic. Everyone in the middle school knew that Gillian Warring, the Sarah Bernhardt of the eighth grade, was going to marry Mr. Weeks. Even Tim Weeks knew of Gillian's plans. He had seen Gillian in the lunchroom looking at him as she spoke, insisting on herself. *I am. Watch me.*

He is so cute! from the entire eighth-grade class.

Mrs. Archibald, head of the middle school, told Mr. Weeks that Gillian was too smart for her own good. Mrs. Archibald liked best the girls who still wore undershirts and read mysteries. If not mysteries, then something funny. Funny. As far as Mrs. Archibald could see, funny did not much enter into the English department's curriculum. Had Miss Mazur ever considered reading Wodehouse? Why did Miss Mazur insist on that depressing *Lord of the Flies?* Mr. Weeks, on the other hand, loved P. G. Wodehouse. He liked mysteries and crosswords, Scrabble and show tunes. He knew a lot about *Jane Eyre* because the eighth-grade girls read it every year, and they told Tim Weeks about it. They told him they did not think, as Miss Mazur thought, that every object was phallic. That was a sexy word to know, wasn't it? Some of the eighth-grade girls believed Miss Mazur was oversexed, and some of them believed she was really sex starved!

Tim Weeks told the girls he didn't want to hear them disparage their teachers.

"*Disparage?* What does that mean?"

"We weren't bad-mouthing her."

"It's true though, Mr. Weeks. All we talk about are the sex parts."

"Sex, sex, sex. Why do you girls think you can talk to me like this?" Tim Weeks asked these eighth-grade girls, and they said, "Because," and laughed. They had trailed him in school and out of school, girls past and present. Mr. Weeks! The best!

"Do you like the present sixes better than you liked us?"

"You never liked us, Mr. Weeks. Admit it!"

"You don't like us anymore."

"That's right," Mr. Weeks said. "I like the others better."

Ha-ha-ha, from all the eighth-grade girls, who said, "You love us, Mr. Weeks. Admit it!"

"Mr. Weeks, be careful you don't disappoint anyone by marrying."

Anna Mazur saw him surrounded by sixth-grade girls and eighth-grade girls, all of whom seemed to be teasing him at once for his new tie, the blue tie with hot-air balloons that he said was a gift from his mother. When he smiled, the under-folds of his eyes turned down sweetly. Anna Mazur watched as students pressed him, circled about, said, "We'll get you some elf shoes, Mr. Weeks."

The middle-school girls laughed and laughed, but ask what seniors had thought of middle school, and they gagged and howled and said it was the worst time of their lives. Older girls would say they didn't laugh much in middle school, but here was middle school in front of Anna Mazur. Middle-school girls laughing; middle-school girls, an acquired taste, an age of elbows and knees, at once knockabout and full of shyness, streakers on the sleepover, always out of fashion, over- or under-dressed—here they were laughing. Middle-school girls: Anna Mazur did not really love them, but Tim Weeks did and his love was returned.

If you asked a Siddons girl what a Siddons girl was, she invariably replied, "We're nice."

"Different ones of us taught different chapters."

"That's an idea."

"He assigned us."

The eighth-grade girls were giving Miss Mazur suggestions.

"Why can't we read a book like *To Kill a Mocking-bird* again?" from the same blinking back of the room, Gillian's constellation.

Marlene

Marlene sat at the foot of Astra's bed and talked about school. Marlene reported on what she was listening to in the senior lounge. The Billie Holiday that Ufia put on with a flourish, the Rolling Stones, Smashing Pumpkins. Music was school, the best of it for Marlene, although she had graveled her voice with smoke. What else had Marlene been listening to? What stories? Edie Cohen was wild for Brad Pitt and had his face all over the walls in the senior lounge. Ufia said, "Why do you have to have these idiot movie stars all over the lounge?"

"Ufia is such an intellectual," Astra said.

What else was there to say? Suki and Alex looked for Will Bliss every weekend. "But you knew that already. They think he's still not back at boarding school. For a while they thought he might have been kicked out, but they couldn't find anyone reliable enough to confirm it. Mondays we get the Bliss Report. It's boring." What else? "Dr. Meltzer is expecting a baby."

"He has a dozen kids already."

"Sarah Saperstein says it's humanizing. Whatever that means."

"She would know."

"She's his pet." And? "You probably already know this," Marlene said. "Lisa Van de Ven and Miss Wilkes."

Astra made motion of a *yes.* Lisa Van de Ven and Astra Dell were in Dance Club together, and in that way were friends, but Marlene had to tell Astra. After all those years, years of hurts, middle school especially, eighth grade. *Why would Kovack think to ever come up to us?* Lisa to her gang. Astra had not been in anyone's gang; she had been, was still in a way, exclusive with Car Forestal.

"Do you talk to her?"

"Lisa?" Astra said.

"Car."

"Yes."

"She's never in the lounge."

"Car studies a lot at her dad's. It's quiet there. It's like being on the moon. Everything floats and looks romantic. There is no dust there whatsoever."

"No dust," Marlene said. "I'm shedding all the time," and she only had to look down to find a long strand of hair somewhere on her person.

Astra said, "Me, too." She said, "Not now, of course," and she laughed. The truth of it wasn't horrible or it was; only Astra was determined to get better. "I have faith," she said. "I have a community behind me. A lot of people visit—you among them—and it makes a difference." The doctors were applying things, and their cruelly mechanical equipment still hurt, silvery and sharp and cold; the machinery made her shake and run, want to run away, tear the IV from her arm, run open armed to sleep. "I'm waiting for the day when I wake up and feel nothing but a pleasant consciousness. I used to wake up that way. In Car's father's apartment, I didn't feel my body at all. That's what a perfect place it is. Maintained but unlived in for months at a time."

Siddons

Astra Dell and Car Forestal, for all of their temperamental differences, had been best friends since nursery school. Suki and Alex were baby birthday party friends. (Suki said anyone she met after sixth grade did not count as a friend.) Kitty Johnson and Edie Cohen turned exclusive in their tenth-grade year on Swiss Semester. Sarah Saperstein and Ny Song were nerds in love. They admitted it! They had the same favorite classes, the same favorite teachers. They thought Dr. Meltzer was funny and trailed after Dr. D asking about Catullus.

A lot of students loved—they used that word often, generously, fervently—they absolutely loved Miss F. Miss F was kind and accessible. She made math almost interesting even for the weaker students. She held math contests that carried prizes of bags of jelly beans and chocolate Kisses. Other teachers were kind. Mrs. Nicholson was especially forgiving of late papers and absences, and Mr. Philips was known to offer makeup tests in history. Miss Hodd—who taught the creative writing elective, as well as tenth-, eleventh-, and twelfth-grade English—had a dinner last June and let her seniors drink sangria.

Kitty Johnson was on a student panel for prospective Siddons parents, and along with Sarah Saperstein and Ufia Abiola, she spoke about the best of the Siddons experience, which included remarks on "the support and affection students feel from their teachers." Kitty read from a talk she had used before. "I never considered myself a 'mathy' person simply because I hated fractions with an unhealthy passion. So it took me by surprise when my physics teacher suggested that I pursue the Advanced Placement course in senior year."

Miss Brigham sometimes remarked on how many of the teachers gave over weekends to class trips and social service projects and fund-raising fairs and baseball and basketball and badminton contests. She did not mention the chaperones needed for the chorus trips. Miss Brigham also did not remark on Miss Mazur's visits with Tim Weeks to Astra Dell. She did not know about them any more than she knew about Mr. Rhinelander's generous habit of slipping Greta Varislyvski, his genius chess player, a twenty for a cab after tournaments. *Keep the change* was his message.

Miss Brigham didn't know that Mr. O'Brien was in love with Kitty Johnson and that he told her of his love every time they met in advisory. He got mad at Kitty, too; they had fights. Kitty didn't always show up for their meetings. "Imagine," Kitty had told Edie, "imagine the intensest sex without sex, and that is my relationship with Mr. O'Brien." Wednesday advisory they sat together at a lunch table pressed against the wall and talked. Sometimes they talked for hours after school. Mr. O'Brien sometimes cried. He had a young wife and a baby in New Jersey.

"He is exhausting," Kitty said. "After all my applications are in, I'm going to put my life in order."

Miss Brigham did not know about Kitty Johnson and Mr. O'Brien. She was not a woman for romance; she liked emotional business kept at home. What would she have said to Mr. Rhinelander's *Keep the change, Greta?*

"Keep the copy of *The Scarlet Letter*." Miss Hodd said as much to any girl who seemed halfway interested in any book in her homeroom bookcase. "The school has more than enough copies, and you should read it." School was ongoing Christmas: something always to take home. Lost-and-found freebies could be had at the end of every term, and early birds to the table of clothes could sometimes find expensive labels. One year Marlene Kovack went home with a black Nicole Miller blouse—surely someone's mother's. There were fleeces and scarves and gloves and sweats, umbrellas and flip-flops and pencil cases, all unclaimed and free to student and teacher shoppers on the last day of school before the holidays. The rule was that if a student later recognized an item as being hers, she would have to think of it as still lost or else negotiate for its return.

Part of the experience of school was the daily reward: rewards of flattery and affection, signals of success, prizes, gold stars and smiley faces, exuberant marginalia on essays and tests—*very smart, insightful, terrific, exactly, yes, yippee!!!!*

Siddons

Alex had her camcorder on yearbook's lit editors and "guest editors" gassing in the lounge. *Wallowing in their wit* was how Suki put it. Why was Suki there? She stuck her face up close to the camera and said, "I am contributing."

One of the two Elizabeths, Elizabeth G., was telling her own significant teacher story. Fifth grade and for some reason she couldn't do her history homework. "So Miss Bell stapled my hair." That was good. Everyone agreed they should use that on the "Indelible Memories" page. Definitely. Worst academic experience? "Too many," Alex said, "they blur." Edie said, "The most grief I ever got out of an assignment in high school was definitely tenth grade's research paper. Having the most obscure topic imaginable, mathematical achievements in non-Western cultures during the Renaissance, made it worse."

"I didn't really like my topic either," Alex said, "but I got stuck with it. Calvin's Geneva. I couldn't figure out what my thesis should be."

"That's a problem," Kitty said.

A Daughter

Re: Dance Concert seniors
To: Katherine Johnson
cc: Ufia Abiola, Edwina Cohen, Alex Decrow,

Krystle Cruz, Suki Morton
Astra Dell isn't up to choreographing a dance.
Not really. We should be prepared to finish it
for her.
Any thoughts? Be realistic.
Lisa

Re: Dance Concert seniors
To: Katherine Johnson
I'm really, really sad that we didn't get around to
making a dance with Astra. She's too sick to ask
now. I feel awful, then I wonder what must Astra
feel?
Edie
P.S. Lisa dropped the ball.

Re: Dance Concert seniors
To: Lisa Van de Ven
cc: Ufia Abiola, Edwina Cohen, Alex Decrow,
Katherine Johnson, Suki Morton
Astra Dell is probably writing an amazing book
about life in the hospital bed with an IV and
pale clothes with tiny flowers on them.
xoxoxoxoxo
Krystle

Re: Dance Concert seniors
To: Lisa Van de Ven
cc: Edwina Cohen, Alex Decrow, Krystle Cruz,
Katherine Johnson, Suki Morton
Ladies,

I wish you would all stop being so ghoulish. Astra
is in a treatment that razes the disease, so of
course she looks like hell, but she is strong. She
has a strong heart and a will to live, and we should
celebrate that drive with a dance in her honor, one
of the dances in the program, the most joyous and
energetic dance. My dance might be appropriate.
Ufia

Lisa turned away from the computer and looked up
at Miss Wilkes. They were in school, so it was *Miss
Wilkes.*

"Ufia is so conceited, isn't she?" Lisa asked.

"Are you surprised I found you?"

"No." Lisa turned back to the computer screen.

"Why didn't you show up yesterday?"

"I told you." Lisa logged out and went on talking to
the dark screen. "I forgot." She turned to Miss Wilkes.
"Don't act like my mother."

"What I don't understand is, how could you forget
when you made the date yourself?"

"How? I'm applying to college, that's how. I've got
February deadlines. What's the big deal, anyway? I forget all the time. I know who you want me to be, but I'm
a little screwed up."

"You're more than a little because it's not just yesterday, and you are the one who insists we meet. Wasn't
that you last night in tears?"

And when the girl didn't respond, Miss Wilkes spoke again, in a gentler voice. "I know it's hard to be kind," she said, "but it wasn't hard to begin with." Miss Wilkes was speaking as Janet, as a woman in love, untitled, unembellished, a woman with wide hips in peg-legged pants and some kind of scuffed-up loafers. This woman said, "I don't know. You tell me. We don't have to meet. "

"No," Lisa said, "I know. I'm sorry."

Miss Wilkes felt as if she were passing through curtains of feeling. "I'm in a bit of a swoon here, but if you don't want to see me anymore, and you're not in any of my classes next semester—" Miss Wilkes began, but Lisa interrupted.

"I don't."

Miss Wilkes stepped back just as Alex and Suki tussled through the door into the computer room. The girls stopped shouldering each other when they saw Miss Wilkes and Lisa alone at the other end of the room.

"Look," Lisa spoke impatiently, "could we not do this here?"

"Here's as good a place as any." Miss Wilkes stood between Lisa and the two girls, but her voice was growing louder. "We can talk here."

Lisa appraised her. Lisa stood up and hitched her book bag over her shoulder and said, "You just said we didn't . . . ," but even before Lisa had finished, Miss Wilkes had begun to move away. Suki and Alex watched

Miss Wilkes and Lisa, and when Miss Wilkes, in the doorway, dared to look back at them, Suki and Alex were still watching. They were smiling.

Suki and Alex

"Where's my camcorder when I need it?" Alex said. "Let's go after."

"I told you ages ago," Suki said. "I told you I saw them on York. They had to be coming from the hospital."

"When did you? Why did you? Oh god, oh god, oh god, oh god, oh god"—Alex, in the middle of the empty hallway, hopped as if she had water in her ear. She was making goofy expressions and Suki was laughing. "I mean it. I don't know what I'm doing half of the time. What am I doing? Where's my camcorder?"

Dr. Meltzer, looking down the hall at Suki and Alex, said, "Why haven't the two of you been shot yet?"

They stood on the landing to the fifth floor and discussed what distinguished them, Alex and Suki, from people like Lisa, from most of their classmates really. They were, both of them, naturally thin. Thin to begin with. "Absolutely no cellulite, Alex." They were distinguished by their slender bodies and their disregard for their bodies, their purebred bone structure, their incongruously elegant good looks, also their money, their snobbery, their wayward society swagger. They pushed

their names together saying, "SukiandAlex, Alexand-
Suki, we're perfect. That's why Meltzer can't stand us."

Suki and Alex were late to class meeting.

"I thought we did this in October," Suki said when she
saw they were nominating speakers for commencement.

"We did," whispered from the floor. "She canceled."

Alex made the same suggestion she had made in
October. Why not Al Pacino? Somebody had to know
him.

"Great!" from the room. The same response made
in October.

Suki said, "He'd be so great!"

Ny Song said, "Who we pick says a lot about us."

"Yeah," Alex said. "It says we like sexy actors, older
men."

"Yeah."

"Al Pacino is hot."

Other suggestions were Sarah Saperstein's uncle,
who happened to be a very important doctor at Sloan-
Kettering, and Patricia Friebourg, an art historian at
NYU, best friend of Edie Cohen's mother, and part
owner of the Friebourg-Johannasan Gallery on Mercer.
Someone called out, "Brad Pitt!" and there were other
suggestions for anyone with only one name. Miss
Brigham wanted the seniors to know the school had
connections with Verlyn Klinkenborg, and he might
agree to speak at commencement. "Great," Alex stage-

whispered, "but who the fuck is he?" Sarah Saperstein knew just who Verlyn Klinkenborg was; in fact, several of the girls knew who he was. Ufia pronounced, mock grandly, that his prose was pellucid.

"Will you turn the camcorder off?" Ny yelled at Alex.

"She's right."

"Get serious."

"I thought a reminder of who we were, the fat-headed class of 1997, would amuse Astra Dell."

Sarah Saperstein was counting raised hands. Verlyn Klinkenborg was elected.

"Over Al Pacino! Unreal."

"What did you expect?" Suki asked Alex. "We've got a lot of nerds in our class."

"Oh god! I hate my class."

"A little something on meatballs or snow, that's what some guy named Klinkenborg will talk about."

"I just thought of Astra." Astra Dell had not been mentioned in the class meeting. Astra Dell was very sick. The rumors of blazing radioactive rods being sewn into arms persisted. The futureless future their friend faced was horrible, so it wasn't any wonder Astra Dell was a nighttime topic and rarely mentioned in class, not this day, when the class elected its graduation speaker, or in the days that followed when yearbook ads were due.

Mothers

Theta Kovack watched over the island of her station as Max Fuise fought the young woman who had brought Max to his appointment. The young woman repeated that Max was to come home with her. He could not visit his friend. They were loud, and Theta made a hushing gesture toward Max and his sitter and also toward the twins, the brothers Beller, who seemed to have the same crooked teeth and menacing hilarity. To the brothers Theta said, "This is an office, boys, not a playground." Theta called out to them, and they shrugged at her voice: *So what?* All day Theta answered the phone and looked up records and sent out reminders. *Forget your teeth and they will go away.* From time to time, she reprimanded the rowdier children in the waiting room. Often she felt sorry for them, saw the children hopped up on sweets and overloaded with lessons. Their mouths looked sore; but at least they were young mouths, red and wet and young. An old mouth was death. Her own dingy mouth she hoped to keep shut, and Theta never looked directly at Mr. Scott when he came in. How could she? He was at least thirty. He looked like the kind of young man who should have experienced braces and private school, but when he opened his mouth, his family's economies were evident.

Wasn't he ashamed to have braces now? she wondered.

Theta was fifty; she had never needed braces—a blessing—but her daughter, Marlene, had needed them, so that Theta's job was a blessing when just the every-day expenses were wearing. Theta answered the phone and looked up records and sent out reminders and in this way kept up her own modest home and made payments on the money she was borrowing for Marlene's tuition.

Theta made some mistakes in the afternoon; a woman with an expensive camel-colored feed bag on her shoulder questioned the cost of a procedure. Theta was right, but she addressed the woman rudely. Theta penciled in a wrong date, then said it aloud, but a hooded sweatshirt with a mouth brace corrected her. Theta broke her pencil in a passing fury, one of the small rages out of nowhere that beset her; she misplaced a statement; she did not have lunch. Her biggest mistake of the day was when she walked through Bloomingdale's to get to the subway. Weaving through the mezzanine's bazaar could be cathartic and airy, especially in the summer, but in January, clobbered by the weight of her wet winter coat, the perfume halls were oppressively bright; every surface was a mirror, and her skin, she glimpsed, looked patchy and chapped; she felt dirty. Then on the subway, there was only one seat left between her and a young man. She said, "I've been sitting all day," and it seemed he didn't doubt her because he took the seat. She was surprised at his alacrity, and hurt. Someone at the Food Emporium took her place in line, but she was too tired to argue and went down another aisle sure that some product would beckon. She bought midget Brillos and Bounce fabric softener.

Theta's evening at home grew worse.

"Your manners!" Theta said to Marlene when she discovered her daughter had mauled the ice cream she meant to have for dessert.

Dessert already? After the grocery shopping, after the hazardous *whump* of the burners igniting came dinner, but she had no memory of dinner. What did they eat? Had they talked? Theta remembered what she had wanted for dessert was ice cream. After Bloomingdale's came the butter pecan. But what was butter pecan ice cream when all the pecans were missing?

"You've gouged out all the nuts and left a mush."

"I'm sorry."

"I mean really. Your spoon's been all over this. Who's going to want to eat it now?"

"I said I'm sorry."

"But this is a habit of yours, Marlene."

"I'll stop."

"I was looking forward to butter pecan ice cream. I think more than anything else, I wanted butter pecan ice cream tonight."

"Oh, for heaven's sake, Mother"—Marlene pushed away from the table—"get a grip," and she pushed the swinging door open and set it swinging back and forth.

Theta did not move from the table; she stirred the ice cream to milk shake consistency and sipped it to soothe all that was sore. Now she remembered they had talked at dinner about Astra Dell's tooth, how it broke apart and powdered like a clay pot when Astra merely smiled. The kiln of chemotherapy had brittled every part, and she was fragile and feverish. All day Theta saw red, wet, young mouths, rawed by braces and re-tainers and bands, mouths tirelessly open in the way of good health. She did not want to think of a sick mouth, and she numbed her lips with ice cream and forgot the sick girl.

Siddons

The two Elizabeths, yearbook coeditors, told Alex that so far this year's photographs of clubs and sports were clearer than in other years, and what the two Elizabeths had wanted all along were really, really clear pictures and fewer of them on a page. "We don't want another ugly yearbook."

Alex said the book was going to be ugly no matter what they did. "If you'd just let me take candids."

"I don't think you hear what we're saying, Alex."

"Why, what are you saying?"

The two Elizabeths, sturdy students, knew enough not to argue with Alex.

"I don't have to get up too close for group shots," Alex said. "The fat people are always easy to identify."

"Don't we know it," said the two Elizabeths, as alike and plump as pears.

Alex and Suki

"Yearbook ads are the best part of yearbooks, don't you think?" Suki and Alex were sitting on the stoop composing their ad to each other, a full-page good-bye. It was a matter of design. There wasn't any text.

"We've already said everything."

Astra Dell took out an ad for Car, a modest quarter-page ad with a modest photo of two girls in front of a modest house. The girls are arm in arm in bathing suits. More text is on the page than photo. A long quotation from Virginia Woolf.

> How then, she had asked herself, did one know one thing or another thing about people, sealed as they were? Only like a bee, drawn by some sweetness or sharpness in the air intangible to touch or taste, one haunted the dome-shaped hive, ranged the wastes of the air over the countries of the world alone, and then haunted the hives with their murmurs and their stirrings; the hives, which were people.

———

Quirky the college counselor told Alex, "I'm going to mention your senior page in my letter to RISD. It's terrific." Ufia, looking on, agreed.

On a white page, pleasing margins, was a dark cube made up of two pictures of Alex. The pictures were arranged so the little and the big versions of Alex looked to each other; everything converged in a satisfying cube reminiscent of a Rubik's Cube. One version of the two Alexes had been printed in some tricky way and looked silvered.

"Looks modern," Ufia said. She read the quotation. "Serious," she said.

"It was going to be Nirvana," Alex said. "I was going to have 'I think I'm dumb, or maybe just happy,' but then Suki showed me the Toni Morrison."

Lisa looked at Kitty Johnson's senior page and pronounced it as good as Alex's page. Better for its simplicity. A mirror image of herself in a deeply shadowed modest profile. Lisa said she looked like Grace Kelly, which pleased Kitty because she did look like her— white blond pretty—and because Grace Kelly was one of Kitty's crushes. She and Edie were also obsessed with Jackie O. They had made Kitty's mother pull over to the side of the road in the country when the radio announced Jackie Kennedy Onassis had died. Edie and Kitty got out of the car and ran into a field and shouted and cried until Mrs. Johnson threatened to drive away. Kitty bought up all the magazines from the time.

Kitty's yearbook picture had blue shadows and a quality like pearl.

"I guess it says it all about each of us, yes," Ufia said, standing just behind. Ufia saw everything; she was the ultimate layout editor.

After the table of contents came the dedication. This year to Miss Hodd. Then a picture of the staff section and explanation of the theme. This year detectives. Alex in the picture is wearing dark glasses; Ufia, a beret. The background—a brownstone stoop, a bare tree—looked rained on. They carried umbrellas. "With perseverance and craftiness, we've uncovered every mystery and solved every problem we encountered along the way at Siddons." Next page a double spread of baby pictures with clues to each baby's identity; then a "Remember When" section. The two Elizabeths, already fleshy, smiling in a tropical setting at a booth eating ice cream; Kitty as Amelia Earhart on Famous Women's Day; then the in-crowd again, Alex, Suki, Car, Astra, Kitty—the five of them seated on the edge of the stage, legs identically crossed, hair identically swooped to one side, long, side parted. Only the tights and tops are different. Astra is the smallest. A steeple of pictures had girls in twos, in school uniform, in party dress, and in costume.

"Who's the sexy six-year-old with the cigarette holder?"

"Alex?"

First-grade or second-grade class picture, all the girls with two hairstyles: pulled back or side parted. Ufia's is the only black face then; her hair is elaborately, tightly braided. The sisters and the cousins and the aunts in straw hats: Gilbert and Sullivan, seventh grade.

Alex took a half page and Suki took the other half to congratulate each other on surviving without Will Bliss and, it seemed, without parents. Where were their mothers and fathers? Only Mrs. Morton's arms appeared in one of Suki's ads holding out a cake with one enormous candle erupting from the middle. Under the photograph Suki had captioned: "Everywhere phallic!" Arrows, a small map of upper Park Avenue, pictures of the entranceway to 1088. A smudged head of what might have been a boy. More arrows. "The minute she walked in, Minta had her glow"—from Suki again. Alex's message is "Smootchies." Even in black and white, the evening dress-up pictures from this year seemed lit up, two sticks in spangled tubes, Suki and Alex, bright as beads.

Numbers

❦

Siddons

"Eighty-eight days of school until graduation!" This announcement, made by Suki and Alex at morning meeting, was greeted with a barbaric yawp from the class of 1997. So that was exciting, and after morning meeting the rumor that Astra Dell had been given an orange wig was confirmed by Marlene Kovack of all people.

Alex asked Ny Song if she had considered Astra Dell in picking the commencement speaker. Was it a good idea really to have a cancer specialist?

Ny Song said she had thought of Astra. She thought that to have Dr. Saperstein (because Verlyn Klinkenborg was unable to attend) would show people how the class has always confronted reality.

"Oh please," Suki said.

"His career is inspiring." Ny did not look at Suki but continued to address Alex. "We haven't forgotten Astra."

"How could we? We're reminded all the time," Krystle said.

Alex said to Ny, "If we're trying to show people how we confront reality, Dr. Saperstein should be Cum Laude speaker, not commencement." Alex smiled. "Cum Laude is reality; then you find out who is smart in the class. And you, Krystle, are not in the group."

"You say awful things, Alex."

"I just say what everyone else is thinking, Ny."

Suki exhaled through her nose to get the smoke out fast. "You dope," she said in a smoker's tired voice, a deep voice that sounded much like her mother's. "Think of it: Saperstein, Abiola, and Song. Should I go on? Car's a sick A-type, and Kitty . . . you don't get as many migraines as Kitty Johnson does for no reason. We've got a nerdy class. Saperstein, as she will happily tell you, got an eight hundred in math."

"I hate that girl."

"Don't forget Lisa Van de Ven . . ."

Siddons

The January Math Challenge had three parts:

Part I: Express as many of the perfect squares less than 1,000 as the sums of two or more consecutive integers as possible. Example: $9 = 4 + 5$

Part II: The sequence 2, 3, 5, 6, 7, 8, 10, 11 consists of all positive integers that are not perfect squares. What is the 500th term of the sequence?

Part III: Find the largest positive integer such that each pair of consecutive digits forms a perfect square. Example: The number 364 is made up of the perfect squares 36 and 64.

Saperstein and Song both said it was easy.

"Then why don't you answer it and get a bag of M&M's?" Alex asked.

"Because we helped make it up."

CHF

The trouble with writing at age seventeen was Car already knew her work was juvenilia. Nevertheless, she hoped to win the Selfridge this year. Of all the seniors, the prize for four years of excellence in English would surely go to her, wouldn't it? Astra was out of the running; she was sick, and Kitty Johnson was her only competition, but O'Brien might feel guilty promoting his pet. Also in Car's favor was *Folio;* she was editor of the upper-school literary magazine, and a poem of hers had appeared in an anthology, *The Best from the High Schools, 1996.* But what appeared in the anthology was juvenilia, wasn't it?

At least Car wrote to Astra. She wrote letters and some of them she sent. She wrote sincerely; she considered how it felt to be unwell—and didn't she know unhappiness herself? Her mother in her sable coat on her way to some disappointment—wasn't her mother enough to be sad about? But it was a tawdry suffering compared to Astra's condition. What Astra had to be sad about also brought wisdom. For Astra, what to care about was clear and large. For Car, it was just this stupid problem:

$$y + y + 3xy + 10x = 12$$
$$\underline{dy} + 2y\underline{dy} + 3x\underline{dy} + 3y + 10 = 0$$
$$dxdxdx$$
$$\underline{dy}(1 + 2y + 3x)5 - 3y - 10$$
$$dx$$
$$\underline{dy} = -\underline{3y - 10}$$
$$dx(1 + 2y + 3x)$$

Marlene

Marlene asked, "Is it okay if I just sit here until she wakes up?" The nurse didn't see why not, so Marlene sat away from the bed with her feet tucked under her, doing math on her haunches. When she had finished the last problem, she stood and stretched and walked around Astra's room. She opened the closet door and touched the few clothes she had touched before. She studied the photograph of Astra's ruffled mother in pearls. "No sir"—from Marlene, talking to herself, looking through Astra's basket of mail for something new and finding old Car Forestal. Her tiny handwriting had an insect delicacy.

> . . . *You can't stop this. All you can do is pretend to be sad that you are leaving and smoke your medicine and hide your skill as if you are ashamed, but I know that you are happy this way. The only thing you have to excel at now is leaving, because you only get to once.*

Marlene put Car Forestal's letter in her backpack. She put away her math book, too, and began the noisy, effortful business of dressing for winter. Marlene looked at Astra. "Wake up," she dared. She wanted Astra to see her at the end of the bed: surprise! She was in Astra Dell's company as she had never been before. Before was only looking on and most often from a distance, glimpsed: the unexpected prettiness of Astra's bare feet braced against the ribs of the rowboat. Washington trip, eighth grade, years ago. Now the smallest, slenderest feet she had ever seen were covered. Her feet were covered, but her bald head was laid bare. The horrible wig on its stand was wrong, and Marlene-at-the-bedside was part of the wrongness in the room, yet she was here, wasn't she, the insistent visitor wisping smooth the folds and wrinkles in the sick girl's bed. How swollen and dark and dirty were Marlene's hands compared to the thin cake of soap that was Astra's hand outside the covers against her face turned away, body in the fetal position. How could such a face as Astra's be let to leave this earth and a criminal's allowed to stay?

Fathers

Mr. Dell left his desk with not so much as a paper clip on its surface. He was a carefully groomed man and a long, loose stroller; he did not seem rushed even when he said he was rushed. "I'm late," he said to no one in particular as he scanned the kiosk's magazines. The headlines blurred. "My daughter's going to wonder where I am." He looked at the candy selection, too, until the number six uptown came through. On the subway he stood and watched two teenage parents, a heavy girl and a slight boy, and their child in an inflated snowsuit. The boy was offering orange chips to the child, who licked off the color and sucked each chip. The child's mouth was unnaturally orange, which did not wash away when the boy spilled Coke into the child's mouth. The boy was clumsy but happy to be feeding his family. He smiled. He offered Coke to the girl, but she refused. "With all that slobber on the can?" she said. The bemused boy and his sullen girl and their child—sexless in a snowsuit—did not get off the train with Mr. Dell but went on traveling north.

On the street again the quiet snowfall was growing noisy. This was the storm they had predicted, and those readied for inclemency hucked open their umbrellas, and he ducked, he weaved, he dodged umbrellas. He had to get there fast through the arc of the hospital entrance-way, past the purposeful, the dumbstruck and adrift. He used his long legs. Corridor C, elevator three to the fourteenth floor and sick children. Corner bedroom, view of the river.

He slid his hand along the railing of his sleeping daughter's bed as he walked toward the window and saw the agitated river below. He was still in his topcoat, he was dressed for the weather, and the weather was exciting. The snow, at a hard angle, was falling fast; parked cars, railings, sidewalks, street trees were all on their way to being beautiful.

Astra was asking, "Is it cold in here, Daddy?"

Ever since the red-hot rod treatment had ended, Astra was almost always cold.

He couldn't tell if it was warm or cold in the room. He wasn't melting anymore, but he was damp. He said, "It's snowing outside." He said, "A big storm is on the way. They're talking over a foot."

Astra was unimpressed; she was falling asleep again. "Marlene Kovack steals my mail."

"What?" But when he turned back to look at her, he saw the sleep that veiled the drugged was drawn across her face. Now he could tell himself she was in for the night; Astra was home. Home: a shoe box of cards, letters, plants, stuffed toys, and photographs framed or pasted on construction paper. Many of the same girls who came to visit at the hospital were in the photographs with Astra. Car, Suki and Alex, the same girls he once found hiding with Astra under the dining table.

An only child pranks her parents alone. He had said this to Grace—why? His was a depressed view, wasn't it? Wasn't it—look at the picture of the girls, all mischief, in collusion with his daughter to break her out of this place.

Survivors. Twelve years together at school. The girls had taken the survivor picture for the yearbook in Astra's room and sent her a copy with attached commentary. *Remember: Kum Bah Yah in D.C., Suki's chicken walk, donut holes . . .*

He didn't like the photograph: all those fleshy faces—even Car looked fat pressed next to Astra's bantam skull.

Car had made it to the hospital for the photo session; her second visit since Astra had taken ill. (What was the matter with that girl? But Astra had kept her beatific smile; she never betrayed Car's secret, whatever it was, though Mr. Dell suspected it had to do with Car's father.)

Mr. Dell draped his coat and scarf over the back of a chair and sat at the foot of his daughter's bed. He reached for Austen on the window ledge and thumbed to a worn spot.

The hateful Mrs. Norris, sponging pheasant's eggs, was traveling back to Mansfield Park with parcels from the day—a cream cheese, a pretty heath—from Mrs. Rushworth's estate.

The nurses on the floor were kind.

One of them, he saw, had put an extra blanket on Astra's bed. Astra must have asked.

"Astra?"

He pushed up his reading glasses. He wanted to say, "Wait until the troubling part in Portsmouth," but he shut the book on his finger and moved to sit across from where Astra slept, a hillock in the snowscape of her bed. He spoke into her ear. "Wake up, sweetheart. I'm only here for a little while," and that is when he noticed how hot she was, and then he called the nurses and then his daughter began to shake violently. He watched; he stood by, stood aside as others—a blur of nurses, an intern, a doctor?—moved around her bed, and her fever spiked to 107 degrees; it spiked and lasted for quite some time. There was the code chart as proof, and all the while Astra was making delirious jokes in the strong arms of her nurses, saying, "I'm going to spend my life shaking in a rocking chair." An allergic reaction someone was saying. Mixed donor platelets. None of what they were saying made much sense, and Mr. Dell was shaking himself to see his daughter so silly in her pink delirium; it made him cry to hear her cackling, crazy jokes: "I'm rocking!" She sounded like her mother, like her mother's mother and all those sly beauties with their corn-crackle laughs and drawling voices: "A good attitude is like kudzu, darlin', it spreads."

Dance

Fathers

She should have died that night, but David Dell shook harder than even his daughter—in confusion and rage and fear. He shook, he stood, he sat, he knelt near enough to his daughter's bedside and prayed, and the girl went on living. His own hair, he was sure of it, had grayed, whereas Astra's was just showing itself; she wore a bandanna.

She was up; she was out of bed; she was home. An outpatient! After great suffering and burning of the body, a quiet descended, *remission*, a word to be whispered, perhaps not yet used; besides, someday, years from now, sudden and cruel, it always came back, didn't it? Cancer, blunt, done in a matter of weeks, months— never more than a year; the second time around it came fast. David Dell had heard the histories at the funerals before. In ironic, doomsday voices, the closest friends were glad to recount when the big C struck finally. *He was planning their vacation when his arm began to hurt . . . That was six weeks ago; now he is dead.* How it happened:

this healthy man or that strong woman, and who would have guessed? *Who could have known? That time we went fishing was our last . . . or . . . Not so long ago we were at her daughter's wedding.*

And how did Astra Dell look? She was very thin; she wore dark clothes; she often whispered when she talked. She said, "I still get tired very easily."

Her father said he had known all along she would get well. He said what he thought Grace would have said, that he had always been sure of Astra's recovery, convinced of it from the beginning, as who could imagine such a girl as this to be extinguished so young? No, he insisted he had always believed she would get well. In truth, he had mostly expected her death to arrive as her mother's had, mercilessly. Nothing he could do, nothing he could do, and he would offer up his life for Astra's; he was ready to take on her disease, whatever it was. He had never fully understood Dr. Byron. To stand in almost any corridor of the hospital was to stand in a cleaned-out closet with a lot of unused metal hangers jangling. That's what it had felt like to him, and all of the flowers and imported decorations, posters, teddy bears and photographs, the schoolbooks and books for pleasure, a deck of cards, a game of Scrabble, a computer—nothing could change the room where his daughter had slept for half a year. Penitential furniture, hose down, easy to clean. Mr. Dell had rarely sat in Astra's room but stood leaning against the window even

when he read to her. Reading to Astra had been a pleasure he was sure to miss, but he would not miss Dr.
Byron's dull blows—"She is young; her vitality works
against her; the cells thrive." Dr. Byron's dour view of
his daughter's future: *no guarantees, no guarantees.* For
now Mr. Dell was saying, "My daughter is at home."
Whose business was it, besides, to know more? "My
daughter is at home, thank you," Mr. Dell said to all the
well-wishers, and there were many.

Marlene

The changes in Marlene Kovack had happened slowly
over several months, so that her mother didn't notice
until after Christmas that Marlene was in perfect uniform. (All those detentions of tenth grade over the Goth
look Marlene had perfected.) Now the white shirt was
white and very girlish, round collared, soft. Now Marlene wore dark tights, and her shoes were simple and
thin heeled, no longer threatening. Alone of all the seniors, Marlene was taking notes in near-perfect uniform, eschewing a second-semester senior's freedom to
come to school every day out of uniform. Why? "It's
easier," she said whenever asked. Marlene had reviewed
for exams with Astra and had done well. Marlene was
not dumb after all; she had only been lazy, as some of
her teachers had always suspected.

(She hadn't thought of herself as lazy, only bored and alone.)

Was she as smart as Astra? This was a question Marlene asked herself, and though her answer was no, she was not as smart, Marlene nevertheless felt she was like Astra, growing ever more like Astra. Astra had faith; miracles were possible. On her near death, the crazy fever that might have caused brain damage, Astra said, "All I know is that the cancer cells were either cooked or my immune system finally recognized what it had to do. The scans before the fever showed new growth and after showed nothing.

"I don't want to fall behind." Astra said, "I've had to give up on AP calculus."

She sat up straighter and shook her head. After the hivey heat and hurt of chemo, she believed she was getting better. Clean of cancer, she believed. Faith and love and her mother's watching over her. "She was there."

Astra said, "I had a community of faith," and by this she meant Walden and the wider Unitarian Universalist communities and its congregants who prayed for her and with her father. She wrote in her college essay, "The leaps of faith that we take as a community or as individuals do not necessarily lead us away from suffering or strife, and they often lead us toward hard work, but they are the risks that enable us to grow, to heal, and to struggle for something better." Was she quoting someone when she wrote, "Just as long as I have breath, I must answer, 'Yes,' to life"? Saintly girl.

The tooth? That happened. Chemotherapy patients often lost or broke teeth. She smiled at Marlene and said, "See? All fixed." Then she said, "You're completely weird, Marlene. Now that you don't have to be in uniform, you're in uniform."

Marlene came forward and bent to the ball of her forehead and kissed Astra and touched the top of her head, Astra in her Joan of Arc hair. Would she let her hair grow as long as before?

"I don't know," Astra said. "Short's awfully easy."

"I am really, really glad you are home and feeling better."

"Best ever," Astra said, and she frowned a little. "Only I get tired," and she shut her eyes, and by the time Marlene reached the door, Astra had fallen back against the pillows of her plump and quilted girlish bed. Marlene could tell by the way Astra was breathing just how deep a sleep it was, and when she turned back to look into the room again, Astra opened her eyes and said . . . What did she say? "Lucky I was sick." Was she talking in her sleep? Did she say, "Don't take my mail, Marlene"?

Marlene walked uncertainly out of Astra's lobby and bumped into others and must have seemed a tourist or a stroller or a stupid, fucked teenager. Sick, sicko, fucked teenager. She was fucked; she felt fucked. She wanted to walk into oncoming traffic.

Siddons

Kitty Johnson said she was glad not to be in Mr. O'Brien's elective but that Mrs. Godwin's Families in Distress class was grimmer than she had expected. *King Lear* was not in the course description. "It's a bummer to start the day with somebody scooping somebody else's eyes out with a spoon or however the guy did it. And the quizzes. I hate to think how many of mine are on the wall of shame in the senior lounge. Besides, we're seniors. Isn't this supposed to be the slack-off, fun part of high school?"

Ufia said, "Some of us want intellectual engagement."

"Wait until you get to Harvard, Ufia. You'll see a lot of engagement then."

"What a dirty mind you have, Alex," Krystle said.

"Rub my back." Suki sat herself between Alex and Krystle, and bumped against Alex, saying, "Would you please rub my back? I'm so sore." And Alex stopped looking at Krystle and pounded Suki's back until the girl said, "Not so hard."

Jade, the dance coach, said, "It's too late now to think of cutting." Instead Jade's finale included each girl giving herself a window.

"What does that mean?"

"If you'd come to rehearsals," Krystle said.

"Bite me."

"Nothing should happen on the extension," Jade was saying to Lisa. "And if you have trouble with the lean and lunging, well . . . Terry will clean up on Monday." Jade looked at the seniors. "If you feel uncomfortable, see me, but I'm not spending hours on any one dance. Those days are gone." Then she circled the room in address. "Every choreographer," Jade said, "you're now a dancer. Hand your dance to your people. Amen. I love you guys."

Kitty said, "Will everyone remember etiquette backstage? Nothing back there belongs to us. Not one bobby pin. It's the drama department's. You've got to organize yourself. Put your gear in a little corner, so you know where your stuff is, all of it."

"The show is less than an hour and a half," Jade was saying to Lisa.

Ufia said, "Seventy-eight minutes."

Krystle walked around the gym with a garbage bag picking up the afternoon rehearsal's refuse, the empty water bottles and candy boxes left mostly by the middle schoolers, she guessed. The coffee refuse was theirs, surely, the juniors and seniors. Upper school's indulgence: expensive coffees from the seafaring shop on the corner, the one with perfect cupcakes and, outdoors, pretty foliage in all the seasons.

"I'm sick of you guys," Jade said to some girls lingering in the folds of the curtain. "Go home," Jade said, but she was not so emphatic, seeming drugged by the hallucinatory nonsense of their nonstop talk now that rehearsal was over.

"Did you know a sneeze travels a hundred miles an hour?"

"A lot of moose or a moose so no fishes."

"But what's the plural of rhinoceros?"

"Oh, Kitty, why so sad?"

Kitty spoke quietly and out of Jade's hearing. "Seniors, don't forget your money for the flowers."

"I'm serious. Chapters nine through eleven in *To the Lighthouse*."

"Oh great! More chapters where nothing happens."

"Don't fret!" Suki jostled against Alex. "We'll stalk Will Bliss," she said, and the two, bumped up against each other, shouldering past the younger girls, lugging stuffed feed bags on their backs.

"I need a suitcase," Alex said. "This is ridiculous. I'm carrying my life."

Fathers

All of the dances had meaning, however difficult it was at times to discern given the distraction of the music, but Ufia choreographed a dance set to a smoky voice in a song about skin color. Ufia and three black dancers—Mr. Dell knew only the seniors—in yellow dresses onstage.

The dance involved something made up to look like a brownstone stoop. The girls changed places on the stoop, but their attitudes were by turns sultry, submissive, dismissive, and independent. The song played these same changes. The next dance involved girls in pajamas—Mr. Dell recognized no one, but his daughter, seated next to him, explained that Gillian Warring, the leggy girl in the blue babydolls, was only in eighth grade, which he took to mean the girl was good, but none of the girls had his daughter's grace. He sat through Alex Decrow's shrill, head-banging solo—"Is she mad?" he asked—and endured "Unbelievable" by EMF and was attentive to even the clumsiest dances, but nothing put him into a gaze, and he was taken aback by Lisa Van de Ven's aggressive movement and wondered at how thin Suki Morton was and why hadn't the dance teacher taken out a few of the weaker dances? His daughter, seated next to him, fully enjoyed herself. After spring break she hoped to come back to school every day—a half a day. "Now and again" was a phrase Grace Dell would have used, but what would she have said to Astra's friend? Car, seated next to her, was too thin by half. The other girl, Marlene Kovack, he knew from the hospital. And in the rest of the auditorium, Mr. Dell saw others from the class. Lettie Van de Ven, of course, was there in the third or fourth row with flowers. She waved at him during intermission but seemed disappointed to see Astra. (Later he wondered if it wasn't the damn wig the woman had been hoping to see.) Teachers came up to Astra during intermission. Mr. Dell recognized Dr. D and Dr. Meltzer and Miss Hodd and Mr. Weeks. The woman from the English Speaking Union contest, that woman, wasn't there; Mr. Dell could not remember her name, but he had seen her at the hospital. Miss Brigham came forward and talked to him: The froth of school goodwill, but Mr. Dell was grateful to the school. His daughter had always been happy in it, and the school returned his daughter's affection. The teachers who visited—and so many had come to the hospital, he couldn't get over it, by which he meant . . . he meant he couldn't get over everything that had happened. He had the sensation that he was standing in the middle of a desolate summer road and that the heat waves, the watery kind a person sees from a distance, were really waves of love, and that he was standing in this water, braced by waves of love from his community—at work, the hospital, Siddons, his wife's church; from all sides came this heat. He hoped never to forget how he had learned to love God, which was what his wife had wanted for him all along. His daughter's near extinction had left him no choice but to have faith.

Mothers

"Oh, for Christ's sake," Mr. Van de Ven said to his wife when she thrust the flowers for their daughter into his

arms at the end of the program so as to catch up with
Mrs. Quirk, the college counselor. The woman was already moving down the aisle, and Mrs. Van de Ven only
wanted to say hello, to say wasn't the Dance Concert
splendid and how hard the girls worked. Lisa was president of dance; of course, Mrs. Quirk must know that.

"You didn't?"

Mrs. Quirk smiled. "Of course, I know."

Mrs. Van de Ven told Mrs. Quirk how glad she was
that the last applications had been mailed off; the tem-
perature in the house was cooler.

"I should hope so," said Mrs. Quirk, who was quick—
she often put these words together—quick Quirk was
quick at turning away.

Poor woman was all Mrs. Van de Ven could think,
but who poor?

A Daughter

The first person Lisa Van de Ven wanted to see after
the concert was Josh, who said he would come, but the
first person she actually saw was Astra, who waved at
her and Jade. All the seniors in Dance Club received
the ritual rose that marked the end of their dancing ca-
reers at Siddons, and most of them were crying. Lisa,
as Dance Club president, received a bouquet as well,
and for this Astra and Car were shouting, "Way to go,

Vandy!" Which was so generous of them considering, considering Astra had been Dance Club president until she took sick. But somebody had to replace her, so Lisa had put herself forward. No one else wanted the job. "Josh!" Lisa shouted out to him, and he bobbed or nodded or whatever boys did. "They're so queer," she said to no one in particular. Damn. Her mother was in the dressing room. "Mom!"

"I'm sorry, I couldn't wait. You were all so beautiful." Mrs. Van de Ven, jostled, backed away from the door, watching. Far-fetched hair, lots of hair, spectacularly flying free of popping hair bands, hair astonishingly clean and glassy. If she could touch it . . .

"Mother, please, we're all getting changed here."

"All right, all right, all right, all right," and she walked out to where the other parents were waiting with flowers.

Lisa said, "Everything looks like shit to me after my mother has seen it."

Marlene

After the Dance Concert, Marlene walked with Car and Astra and Mr. Dell to the corner. Astra was saying she was tired but happy to be out-of-doors in an unaccountably springlike spell—a spring snap—and she feeling springy, though she leaned against her father.

Marlene could not look at him; once before she had been a stranger and now? At the corner the old cut opened: She was not going their way but east, as far east as the river, though she couldn't see it from where she lived. Marlene would have liked to have explained why she stole Astra's mail, but she was afraid. Part of the reason she stole the letters was to ward off being afraid, also curiosity, jealousy. What did Car do for Astra? And the hair clip? The hair clip was to be brought nearer to Astra. It was a comfort for Marlene to hold the barrette in her pocket, the way she might a bit of bone, to caress it and so find strength enough to talk.

A Daughter

"If it's not great sex, and it's not true love, then it's definitely worth my time because how else are you rife with passion and singing with hate all at once?"

Josh said, "Has anyone ever told you, you are a really scary girl?"

"All the time," Lisa said. "So are you interested?"

Siddons

Valentine's Day and Kitty's romantic life amounted to zilch, nada. "All I am doing is counting the days until AP physics is over, and Families in Distress—ha. Oedipus and his brood: our dysfunctional family of the week. I thought second-semester senior year was supposed to be fun." Sometimes Kitty wondered about the Ramsays. Miss Hodd had read the novel with them in junior year; it was one of the books in her elective on heroines. The Ramsays: Were they a family in distress or just a family?

Red sweaters, red tights, bows, bracelets, stick-on hearts, the red streaks of the middle school down the sixth-floor hall were as hectic as the drugstore's cheap displays. The sixth-grade girls had been on countdown since the first of the month, and now here it was Valentine's Day, and Anna Mazur, in pink, was putting an animal valentine on Tim Weeks's desk, this one a picture of a panting terrier with the message: *Be my valentine, doggone it!* His desk was already loaded with big cards from students, homemade some of them, stickers, doilies, pasted-on red hearts: *I'm stuck on you!* A rose, already blackened despite the plastic cap of water on its stem. Some Red Hots, some chocolate hearts, a bag of Twizzlers. Tim Weeks, ever the favorite. She had seen less and less of him since Astra Dell had come home from the hospital, but why did that surprise her when beyond visiting the sick girl, they had never had a date? A few weeks before, she had helped chaperone a sixth-grade outing through the Egyptian wing at the Metropolitan. She had kept her coat on, though it was damp from the walk in the light snow that fell through the elm awning along Fifth. "Bear squares" the girls called the paving stones and skipped, and Anna Mazur had walked behind with Tim Weeks—Mrs. Nicholson was at the head—and Anna admitted, "I've lived here three years now and have not once gone to the Whitney. Isn't that terrible?" He said it was and they had laughed when she admitted the same was true of the Egyptian wing. "I've never been. Don't tell the girls." She stood with him in front of the Fragmentary Head of a Queen in yellow jasper. "How sensuous she is." The wonder of it was the way the face was there in full even as they looked at just the mouth.

Her own mouth was a string of pins. He'd never kiss it.

However did Edie Cohen manage to stick a valentine into every classmate's mailbox when she had been sick most of the week? That was the wonder in the senior lounge, as Edie's classmates discovered their "perfect" individualized, homemade, secretly delivered card with her fat script and XXXXXXXX's.

"This might be my last valentine from Edie ever," Krystle said, and she made a tearful face.

Lisa Van de Ven bought herself a pair of silk embroidered boxers with rhinestones, but she told her classmates the gift was from Josh. In truth, though they had talked and e-mailed, she had not seen him since that night after the Dance Concert when, still in her leotard and gauze skirt, she slid past him into his apartment—"I can't go home. You saw it. My mother's a drunk." She invited him to take a shower with her, but he was smoking up in his bedroom—she could smell it—and didn't answer, so she came out of the bathroom wrapped in a towel, her hand outstretched for a toke, and she said, "I've never had sex with a man, but that doesn't make me a virgin." She said, "Do you have something I could borrow?"

He gestured to the closet behind him. "Help yourself."

She sat with him on the floor; she wore nothing underneath his jeans and soft dress shirt. They smoked. They smoked, and Josh got up to put on something she thought he called *narcotics*, wobbly music that made her sway, but her boobs were bags of sand and her face was doing something ugly. "Oh my god," she cried, and she cried and laughed and cried. "It's all over, I can't believe it, that's the last time I will ever dance on that stage, the last time with any of those stupid people, stupid, stupid Alex Decrow—could you see how we had to cover for her?—oh my god, my boobs weigh a ton," Lisa said, and she went into the bathroom and flung herself into a defeated halter with gymnastic support, and who cared if it was stinky and damp—that stupid stoner Josh was asleep, so where was his hairbrush, didn't he have a hairbrush, where was his hairbrush? "Ach! I look so ugly!"—and she took up a scrub brush he used on his back and banged it against her head. *Everyone has an outstanding feature; yours is your hair.* Her mother said all she needed was a good colorist; all she needed was Elie at Ishi. She brushed her hair and wondered at her face; she knew who she looked like, and it was not her mother. *She's got my hair, at least.* Not her mother's color, never her mother's fake, man-made, fake. "I hate my mother!" *How much does Suki Morton weigh, do you think? . . . How tall is that Ufia Abiola? . . . What does her father research? . . . All those minorities, you know . . . Is she Jewish, is she rich, is she smart, is she Jewish, she must be Jewish, she must be Jewish or Asian. My manicurist's daughter is an anesthesiologist. What are you?*

"'How then, she had asked herself, did one know one thing or another thing about people, sealed as they were? . . . the hives, which were people. . . .' That's such a beautiful passage," Car said when she had finished reading it in the yearbook proof of Astra's ad to Car. The picture of them, girls, arm in arm, in bathing suits. Astra and Car had both wanted sisters, had wanted to be sisters, had pretended to be sisters. In the photograph both girls are missing front teeth, but their smiles make out that the world is hilarious, especially to those with secrets.

What were they keeping from Mr. Dell, who took the picture, and from Mrs. Dell, who stood behind the porch screen at the lake house? How prescient that picture now seemed with Mrs. Dell scratched behind the screen. The picture was years and years ago, if Car were being dramatic, and lately she had been very dramatic. "I called my father to tell him I wasn't coming."

"And?"

"I don't want to talk about it, Astra."

The fantasy of a father, an impeccable appraiser, a cocktail-cool and lethal man with a shapely hand at the small of her back, guiding her through a clamor that seems to lean toward them, toward this man, this pretty father, whose concern is for her—and she? Car is not so demurely dressed as to be expected; the back of her dress is low, and her back, her shoulders, the stem of her neck, the upswept hair, and ears, visible and smally inviting, invite touch, touch, touch, touch, touch. Car, on her knees, put her head in Astra's lap and let the sick girl pet her weeping friend; Astra finger-combed Car's hair out of her face and around the small ear, and thus they sat in Astra's room in a month reduced to dusks. March, nearing spring now and spring vacation, and the enormous old window in Astra's room waggled in the high wind, and the easterly dark was not so complete as to obscure the bombast of the air-conditioning system on the rooftop play yard of the neighboring boys' school. "God," Car said, lifting her head to see how the school's addition had obscured Astra's distant view of the river. "When did they do that?"

"That," Astra said, "was finished just before school started last fall."

"When do the little boys come out to play?"

Mothers

The fat envelope that arrived just before spring break was from Siddons and not, as Theta Kovack had hoped, from the University of Wisconsin. The fat envelope was an invitation to the School Spring Auction and included a list of live and silent auction items and raffle tickets. Top of the live auction list was this: "A fabulous stay for five nights in a beautiful four-bedroom/five-bath private retreat on the island of Kauai, Princeville, Hawaii. The property includes a swimming pool, a staff of seven, and a cook." Next came a walk-on role in a Woody Allen movie, a sleepover for twelve at the American Museum of Natural History, a VIP table at the Hampton Classic Horse Show, a weekend getaway by private jet to Palm Beach and the Breakers, and a day of sailing on a forty-foot Dufour sailing yacht with captain. How tempting to sail away, and there were families that could do just that and did just that, and, to be fair, these same cheerful rich or many of the same also spent their Saturdays at the Family Service Morning, where students and parents could jostle in a good-cause direction: roll pocket change; bead a bracelet for a sick child; decorate and fill a toiletry kit for Women in Need. Time was Theta thought of herself as a woman in need, but Dr. Bickman had hired college consultants for her. (*Theta, how many years have we been together? I know Kal. His kids are going to need braces soon.*) And Kal had come to the apartment and explained the forms: All Theta had to do was . . . and Kal would ink in the final forms, and college was affordable wherever Marlene went. Once or twice, Theta had considered calling Bob . . . but why? *Why bother* was always where she settled late at night when she could almost see the green that was the wider world of college. To think Marlene was about to embark on what she, Theta, had not quite finished. Dentist's receptionist was a good job but not what she dreamed of for Marlene, for Marlene . . . oh something. *What we hope for our students is that each will find her passion.* But friends, one can be passionate about friends; some have a passionate need of them. Not so long ago, whenever it was Astra Dell left the hospital, Marlene had said, "I can't visit Astra at her home. I never went there when she was well; why would I go there now?"

"Those in need can give others purpose" was what Theta had said at the time.

Marlene looked at her as if she had farted, and the girl's expression scared Theta a little for being familiar, and for a few days Theta stayed later at work, didn't want to come home at all. Then Astra called to ask Marlene why hadn't she visited?

Siddons

"'Whoever you are, I have always depended on the kindness of strangers.'" Kitty did a little dance in the lounge.

"Tennessee Williams at last! Families in Distress!" She twirled and fell back onto the sofa. "Now blindness will only be a metaphor."

Astra showed Marlene the mock-up of her senior page and the picture of Marlene that she had found to use— Washington trip, eighth grade, braces. Marlene said, "This makes me want to cry."

"Oh, Kovack!" Astra said.

Marlene said, "I've wanted this," by which she meant her place on Astra's page, there with Miss Hodd and Dr. D, Kitty and Edie, Suki and Alex and Car. Car, Car, Car, the two Elizabeths, Ufia, Ny and Sarah, Mr. Weeks and Miss Mazur. The minister from All Souls, summer cousins in Virginia, her favorite nurse at Sloan-Kettering, Teddy—the little boy with leukemia she loved—Dr. Byron, her horse Lady, Pitiful the cat, and Rye, her mother's dachshund. Grace Dell again and again, Mr. Dell and Mr. Dell. The dog was just a nose.

Astra's quotation was from Emily Dickinson: "'Hope' is the thing with feathers."

Fools

CHF

The front and back covers of *Folio* were black-and-white photographs. The first Car had taken and was of a boy, a slender boy from the waist up, white distance for a landscape. He is not wearing a shirt; his back is to the camera. He is a long-waisted, long boy, long enough to be fifteen, sixteen; cocksure and surely smiling, he clasps his hands behind his back. From youth to old age is the obvious arc of the magazine; an old man reclines on a bed in the photograph on the back. The old man is Alex Decrow's famous grandfather. He looks like Picasso in a lumberjack shirt.

Elsewhere in the magazine were photographs Alex had taken of the old man's house on an island in Maine: an old door ajar, an assuring band of light; light across a ladder-back chair; lace curtains lifted in a window full of light: a clean, hard place. Car, at the literary festival assembly, talked about the photographs in the magazine. She quoted Mark Rothko, who said light was "indeed a wonderful instrument," then, as was custom, she gave the first copy of *Folio* to the head of school, Miss Brigham.

Siddons

"I'm sorry," Lisa Van de Ven said, and Miss Wilkes held out a box of Kleenex.

"I'm glad to talk to you after all this time," Miss Wilkes said. "And I'm sorry, too, but it's not as if Brown's said no. People get off wait lists."

"It's a courtesy."

"You don't know that."

"I do. They took Suki Morton—of course. And Elizabeth F. They never take more than two from our school."

"The competition was stiff."

"I'm smarter than Suki Morton any day," then, "I'm sorry."

"It's okay; it's a disappointment."

The girl's hand was white from playing with a piece of chalk, and she put the chalk down, set it carefully on the edge of Miss Wilkes's table, then turned away to slap her hands over the art room's industrial-size trash can. "I'm sending a check to Wash U," Lisa said. "It's farthest away from my mother." When Lisa turned back to face Miss Wilkes, she saw the chalk smears on her breasts made in the move to clean off her hands. "I'm a mess," Lisa said, and she beat away the dust.

Nothing had changed in Edie Cohen's house. "I'll never be as smart as my brother" was what she said to Kitty Johnson over the phone. "I couldn't even get into my dad's school."

Kitty said, "You have your own talents."

"Really? Like what? And nice doesn't count."

This new Astra was modern. Her hair was an orange fuzz, and she was dressed like a boy in sweatpants and sweatshirt, Dance Club's '97 sweatshirt, still new and stiff. The color looked as if it might flake off.

Marlene said, "You've got the prettiest feet."

"My mother got me hooked on pedicures. It's how I treat myself sometimes." Sometimes Astra sat in a little manicurist's shop on Second Avenue, and Judith did her feet, used a razor, massaged. "She doesn't speak English, but she's very sweet. Only Mrs. Kim speaks English and hers is hard to understand, but she knows who I am from the sound of my voice on the phone. She knows everyone's voice. It's amazing." Astra took a novel with her but always ended up reading gossip magazines. The busy, kitschy covers were in keeping with the whole experience of Pink Roses, next to the deli, a piecemeal salon: wall-to-wall carpeting, three chairs for pedicures, a back room for waxing, some tables for manicures, and a bigger table—big enough for three to sit with their hands and feet slipped into toaster-oven contraptions and there, while their nails dried, to look out at the traffic into the vulgar drugstore across the street. "I think the drug chains are ugly—don't you?" There were little dishes of hard candies on the glass table at Pink Roses and business cards and a photograph of Mrs. Kim with a famous TV newscaster, who was truly cute in a squinched-up way. "I admire people with lots and lots of money who yet know how to save it, don't you?"

Marlene had never had much of an opinion about money. She knew she didn't have as much as many of her classmates. She knew what things cost and could usually distinguish elegant from cheap, but once she had tried on a designer jacket on a walk through Bloomingdale's with her mother, and it had seemed to her then the jacket looked as dingy as a discount. Her body was built for the clothes she was wearing now: tennis shoes, jeans. Car Forestal in her mother's vintage clothes—"the ice-pick toes on her sling-back shoes," Car's description when asked whose. *Manolo Blahnik*. Marlene knew designer names and logos. She had walked through Bloomingdale's with her mother on their way home from Dr. Bickman's office on more than one occasion. She had some polo shirts, but her closets were nothing like Astra's with the rainbow piles in their right cubbies.

"My mother again," Astra said. "Thank you," and she put on the Chinese slippers Marlene handed her. "My mother was a stickler for organization. She had rules. She said etiquette was vastly underrated. My dad said she wrote thank-you notes on their way home from parties." Astra Dell said, "I like that she's everywhere." Then, "Mother helped me pick the colors for this room."

Settled in the window seat in the orangey sediment of the sunset, Marlene saw how the dull roses at Astra's bedside, old sentimental valentines, still shook against the apple-green and white of Astra's room. The right colors for a redhead's room. Oh, that hair. Now was not the time to return the barrette, the same Astra lost at school and Marlene found so many years ago, the one Marlene rubbed in her pocket. Eighth grade: worst year of her life—Dad gone, ugly, loathed. Why did she still feel the need of it, the enormous hair clip, a relic, but she did.

Suki and Alex

Alex said to Suki, "Every time I say Tulane, they say, 'Good party school,' as if I didn't know that."

"They just mean to be insulting."

"Gee, thanks. I never thought of that."

"I don't know, Alex. I don't know what you want me to say."

"Look, I now know how to read and every once in a while I stop and have a thought."

Mothers

At the auction to benefit the scholarship fund, Lettie Van de Ven had bid on and won dinner for six in the sky tower at Daniel's. She had envisioned a celebratory graduation dinner with Nana V. and Marilyn and Paul. Her own mother couldn't fly out from California. That would be a waste, especially since they were all going to California in July, but Bill's sister, Marilyn, was Lisa's only aunt; Paul was a third husband, so he didn't count as an uncle and Lisa called him Paul. *I can't say "uncle." I think I'm being disloyal to Uncle Peter.* Lettie Van de Ven had envisioned a celebratory dinner with Lisa in her graduation dress—the girls still wore white dresses—which if she had any say, and she did have a say, would be a short white dress, and now was the time to be look-ing for one.

"No, I have news for you. We are not buying a long dress. Save that for your wedding."

"There *are* no short white dresses. They're not mak-ing short white dresses this year, Mother."

"Well, we'll have one made, then."

The girl at least had thick hair; otherwise, a bull-dog's body for all her modern dance. Lisa looked like

Bill, and clothes shopping with her had long ago ceased to be fun. She didn't have much in the way of an ankle, a heavy step. Maybe her eyebrows? They were thick and bossy—maybe if they were plucked just a little?

"Mother, will you stop pawing me?"

"I was only thinking you might think about your eyebrows."

"Oh my god."

"I'm sorry. Go in and try it on. I'll wait out here."

"Mother, this looks like a nurse's uniform."

Lettie Van de Ven did what she was famous for doing with her face.

"Okay, okay, okay," Lisa said. "I'll try it on."

When Lisa came out, her mother did that other thing she was famous for doing with her face. "You were right. Now you do look like a nurse."

Unattached

Tim Weeks and Anna Mazur walked a string of girls down Park Avenue to the Alford School to see some of their classmates with the eighth-grade boys from Alford in *Our Town. I've read it too often. It's sentimental. Dated. Old-fashioned.* Maybe, but on this day when Mrs. Gibbs said that "people are meant to go through life two by two. It ain't natural to be lonesome," Anna Mazur saw camels and elephants headed for the ark, and she felt sad. The boy playing George Gibbs had a voice that was soft as a fruit—too much saliva—whereas Gillian Warring seemed never to be surprised. She knew where the play was going and all of its players. "Oh, Mama, just look at me one minute as though you really saw me."

Siddons

The same subjects—Brown and Suki Morton and money—had been part of their conversation so many months ago in the Greek coffee shop. The Mortons were the soup people. Miss Wilkes remembered now. *I'm not a nice girl. I'm growing more disappointed every day.* That was how it had started—*I'm not a nice girl*—and for a few weeks, they had talked after school in the art room. Lisa had come on to her. She had not pursued the girl; rather, she had tried to keep her distance. Tried until she put her hand over Lisa's in the Greek coffee shop. She had put her hand over the girl's, but had she applied any pressure? *You knew I was a take-charge person.* The girl had called her Janet and had asked to visit. School was too personal—whatever that meant—but the single afternoon at her apartment with Taffy all over the place and Lisa's face, the mottled rash, the eyelids plump, reacting on the instant. Allergies. *I think I may only be experimenting, Miss Wilkes.* Miss Wilkes, Miss Wilkes, to be called Miss Wilkes in her own apartment, to be reminded of the awkward self that lurched around the lunchroom every day too early—the trays overturned on the salad-bar selections—too early, so she feigned interest in coffee, which gave her the jitters. She had the jitters in her own apartment. It was cold, of course, on that day in January when Lisa Van de Ven paid a visit, but this shaking came from the ever-hungry self at the teachers' table too early in the morning. *Miss Wilkes, I think I may only be experimenting.* The embarrassment of her appetite, and yet she had learned to restrain herself. For weeks now she had gone to the last lunchtime seating and missed seeing Lisa Van de Ven every time.

Mothers

"I leave you to your own devices" was what he had said on the morning he left, and Theta was late for work. Not the first time she was ever late in all the years— nine years, not so very long ago. The weird thing was that she remembered Bob at the door carrying a yellow suitcase. Theta said to Marlene, "I'm not an imaginative person particularly, Marlene, so this is strange. Don't you think? I see an old-fashioned yellow, a strong yellow, cardboard suitcase. I don't think your father was probably carrying anything. The way I remember it happening he is wearing a gray suit, which also seems preposterous. I can't remember him ever wearing a suit."

Marlene said, "It has to do with maybe the way he wasn't or you wanted him."

"Yes, it does. I know. I don't want to look at his face."

"You miss people more when they're gone," Marlene said while she picked out nuts in a pint of ice cream. "No, that's not how it goes. You—no. People make a big impression on us for not being around, something like that. Astra and I have talked about it." She swallowed. "I love her. She's so great." The carton looked crushed for the heat of her hand, and the ice cream, Theta saw, was a soup when Marlene put it back.

"No one's going to eat that, you know."

"She's a saint. She finds something good in everybody. It's ridiculous."

A girl with a healing touch, true, and for a moment Theta went missing. Something else there was she had meant to tell her daughter, but her daughter was swinging out the swinging door of their old kitchen. Lately it seemed Theta had time, more time to herself, which explained the lightness she felt—better posture—and it was not unwelcome. And the ice cream? Would she miss finding the refrozen melted ice cream with its skim-milk color and consistency? The same she threw away—not for being nutless but because it wasn't sweet anymore, wasn't salty but tasteless—would she miss the trail of her daughter in the house? She didn't know, but Theta Kovack was thinking of going back to school! For what? To finish her degree. And then? Something more.

CHF

The question was why she had included the story that had started as an essay about her father, the one where he sat looking small on a large sofa, with one leg crossed over the other, the leg swinging and swinging the wide bell of his cuffed, creased pants. Everything he wore looked soft enough to sleep in, and the plausive gestures—only his legs were crossed, the rest of him open, his arms opening as if to embrace him or her or him or anyone else who came near—these open arms deceived her, and when she bent to kiss his cheek, he looked into her breasts and said, "Too much French pastry, Carlotta." In front of the Dutch hostess, who knew so many languages and stood just behind in a pleated dress with silken cord, classic as a caryatid, in front of all the elegantly gathered, her father had said she was fat. A fat, bumptious teenager in a too-tight dress unbecomingly thrusting her breasts at the dowagers, at the drab and the dull she had expected to meet and trump. The problem with Car's story was that all the characters were ugly. Even Miss Hodd, who liked

everything Car wrote, had said it was hard to sympa-
thize with a judgmental narrator and discouraged her
from putting it in *Folio*, however accomplished some of
the descriptive passages.

"I wanted to get back at him, of course. I want everyone
to know he's an asshole and a fag." Car said, "I'm sorry."
She said, "I'm just so sick and tired. I'm so mad. I wake
up every morning in a rage."

Nobody wakes up in the morning trying to burn was
what she wrote him.

Car said, "I can't help myself. My only excuse is I'm
young." She said, "Please, don't look at me like that. I'm
serious. Don't make me laugh. I don't want to laugh."

Astra said, "So how was St. Bart's with your mother?"

"I should have gone to Paris and endured my dad."

Mothers

"How does your father feel about Columbia?"

"I don't know why you ask me these things when
you know I don't know," Car said, and she let go of her
knife, stuck upright in the meatloaf, to see if it might
stand. It didn't.

Mrs. Forestal startled. "Damnit, Carlotta," she said.
"Must you?"

Siddons

"Ah," Ufia said, "the sad consequences of culturally motivated depilation."

Alex was sitting on a bag of ice but she was leaking.

"Sit on the floor!" Suki said.

"I can't sit on something hard. I'm in pain!" Alex said. Brazilian bikini wax was the story Alex was telling over and over again to every girl who came into the lounge and asked, "What's the matter with you, what's with Alex, what's with the ice?" *I was at the salon and bored and I figured, why not, but I didn't really know what a Brazilian bikini wax involved.*

Unattached

"Honestly . . ." and then Anna Mazur didn't speak for a long time.

"Honestly, what?"

"I don't know." They were nearing her building, and she couldn't say what she wanted to say because there was so much to say, but here was a chance, and she said, *I don't know.*

"Yes," he said, walking backward away from her door, waving, saying, "Another day, another dollar," saying, "Good luck grading all those papers." And that was how the day ended, walking east on Eighty-second Street, past the barren beds around the twigs that passed for trees on the streets between Lex, Third, Second, First—all the way to her door. Anna Mazur knew what wishing *good luck* meant for her weekend. It meant the papers in her shopping bag, two classes of eight, one of seven, hours and hours of reading until she wasn't sure any more how to spell any word with doubled letters.

"Lucky you," Anna Mazur said to Tim Weeks, "your hands are empty."

Siddons

Madame Sagnier said the seniors in her AP French class were zombies, and she was not alone among the faculty at the class-twelve grade meeting with complaints. Absences, college visits, flagrant infractions, blithely walking down the hall with iced coffees, wearing sandals, wearing very high heels. Girls were late for classes or didn't show up for classes or abruptly left classes.

"They just stand up and leave."

"And you don't do anything?"

Miss F agreed. Some of the seniors were sullen about assignments. "Marlene Kovack, for all the improvements, can still make a face."

"Medusa."

"You know, don't you, what the girls do when they ask to go to the bathroom or when they just arbitrarily exit class? You know? I know. I've asked," Miss Hodd said. "There's a new hand dryer in the third-floor bathroom and they're in there playing with it. It's got jet power to make your skin jiggle."

"Please."

"I'm serious. Sometimes they go back to the lounge and complain about class, or they run errands, print out things for you, Mrs. Quirk."

"They've got college decisions to make."

Dr. D said he had found Alex Decrow in the computer room when she was supposed to be in class. "She said she was trying to get a date for the prom."

"Poor girls," Miss Hodd said. "Some of them have never had a date."

"Ellen," Phil Meeks said. Ellen, her name, Ellen Hodd. "Let's get out of the D's," and he advanced the projector to shine the next report card onto the screen: Forestal.

"What's happening in French, Simone?"

"I told you," Madame Sagnier said. "They're the children of the corn."

Hives

Unattached

Only her small, bare feet, preternaturally pale in black rubber thongs, toes polished, gave away the recently sick part of Astra Dell. The rest of her—in a bush jacket, black jeans, and kerchief—looked armed, alert, and steady. Her red hair was boy-short and spiked, seeming darker, but was it the same color? Astra Dell come back as from up country was how it seemed to Anna Mazur, looking at the girl, happy to see her come to school, and just for the book fair. That was what Astra Dell said. She was on her way to the hospital but stopped at school to find a book to read. This part of getting well took up a lot of hours of every week. How could Astra smile at that, but she did and held up *Anna Karenina*, saying, "I'm thinking it's time for the Russians," and smiled. She read, "'All happy families are alike,'" and didn't bother to finish the sentence; she knew it was famous. "Yes." She said yes to most of Anna's questions: better, every day better, school, some of school manageable, and summer school and then. "I don't know," Astra Dell said. "I'm not sure. And you've had a good year, Miss Mazur?"

Yes, she had had a good year, but some of the best moments were due to Astra Dell's being sick, and she blushed when she talked to the girl, as if Astra Dell already knew how she had brought them together, Tim Weeks and Anna Mazur, but now Astra Dell was an outpatient and—however uneasily—on the mend at home. "And I won't visit her at home," Tim had said. He had said, "I'm actually a very shy person despite appearances. I'm fine around kids, but adults baffle me. I have nothing to say to the girl's father except how fucking sorry I am." In fact, Tim Weeks had been uncomfortable in the hospital, too; he had used the word *obscene* to describe what was happening: "I don't like to look at her"—his words—"and I don't feel comfortable not looking at her. It's *obscene* what's happening on that floor." His vehemence had frightened her, and he had apologized for it. He had said, "Look, I don't want to put myself in a situation where I have to experience death or loss."

"Yes," Anna Mazur said to Astra Dell, "I've had a pretty good year. I like my eighth-grade class." This she said loud enough for her nearby eighth-grade book browsers to hear. "They're very bookish," Anna said, and at that moment in the timely fashion she had about her, Gillian Warring came forward with a question.

"Do you think I'd like this?" she asked her teacher.

"*Lolita* is not what you think it's going to be," Anna Mazur began.

Siddons

"Nothing is," Lisa Van de Ven answered, "nothing is interesting to me or feels useful at all." She was taking three APs and she didn't know why she bothered: Their real purpose was over; she was in college. "When will I ever need to know how to use the antiderivative of a polynomial function to find the area between the curve, the x-axis, and the given bounds?"

Miss Wilkes asked Lisa if she had seen this: And she showed Lisa a painting of a sliver of a face in profile, the slight neck surmounted by the weight of an enormous turban, a bright red towel so carefully painted the fluffy part was visible. Astra Dell's self-portrait. "You could reach out and touch that towel, couldn't you?" Miss Wilkes said. Miss Wilkes looked at the painting with the same wonder she had felt when that poor sick girl—she still looked sick or fatal, didn't she?—when Astra Dell had brought it in. Done at home. Hardly a face, and what little of it there was, was very pale—eyelashes and eyebrows as if done in pencil. The uncertainty expressed in pencil; pencil, so evidently perishable. The towel was in acrylics.

"I could never in a million years paint like that. Do you remember my own self-portrait last year?"

Miss Wilkes remembered.

"I couldn't get my nose right." The nose, the mouth—even the eyes were off—weren't they? Didn't Miss Wilkes think so?

Miss Wilkes thought Lisa Van de Ven was tiresome. "The proportions were off a little, I remember." Miss Wilkes said, "Next time." Next time look at the person you address—meet her eye. Good god, how could this girl have hurt her, but she had—Lisa Van de Ven had made Miss Wilkes's school year unbearably hard for months; she, too, had rubbed her back against the towering wall of *why bother*, and even now she wished the month of May—her favorite month!—were over. She was uncomfortable in Lisa Van de Ven's company, confused, sad, embarrassed. Miss Wilkes had compromised herself to be in this girl's company, and now when she wanted it least, Lisa Van de Ven sought her out! Left notes in her mailbox asking to meet.

CHF

"Places you don't think about on the body hurt," Astra Dell said. "More than hurt, ached. My nostrils dried up and the insides cracked and it hurt to breathe; the tips of my fingers felt swollen; my feet burned. You talk about fever. There was no relief, and I have a low tolerance for pain. I wanted to die. I played the awful game, the one where the people I love are sacrificed so I can live." Astra Dell said, "When I had that allergic reaction and my fever spiked to 107, I was delirious. Then I wasn't asking for anything—my body was clacking on its own—no help from me. I was along for the ride. My father told me. He was there the whole time. He said I was laughing, which is how hard it hurt."

Astra played with the hair-thin pretty silver bracelet Car had given her. "I love this bracelet you gave me," she said. "You know how I love jewelry, but this is the only thing I can wear now. All my other jewels, my rings and bracelets, are too heavy, and they get hot and press against my skin, but this bracelet. I could be wearing a feather. It tickles."

Car said, "How are you feeling now?"

"Tired, relieved. No more dosing after yesterday." Astra said, "I have the weekend to rest and then I am coming back to school." Astra said, "I miss it."

Car asked if Astra wanted some healthful snack, but she did not. Astra said, "The receptor cells in my mouth have been confused by the treatment. Most of what I eat tastes like metal. This is a side effect that passes quickly, I'm told. I want to enjoy food again. Does that surprise you?"

What surprised Car, and she felt it on the walk home, was her own appetite. The expensive coffee shop with its seacoast cottage interior was just down the block, and they made the most astonishing chocolate chip cookies. The glass case of cupcakes and scones, muffins, cranberry-blueberry-walnut muffins, studded nutty crusts, and burst berries. The famous mini-cupcakes, yellow cake with a twisted cap of buttercream frosting, a circus of sprinkles on top. Oh, she was hungry. She was hungry and she could eat, and Astra wanted to eat and Car wouldn't let herself eat, though she could eat whatever food pleased her and it would not taste like a penny, a penny or a key or a mouthful of nails. By the time she reached the expensive coffee shop, she had come up with a long list of metal objects. She was sucking on a doorknob when her turn came to order, and the word that came out was *coffee.* "With skim milk, please." Belt buckle, cuff links, clippers, and cutlery. The easiest way to get the figure you want is to be sick.

Alex and Suki

"Psychosexual," Suki said. *"Psychosexual.* I just like to say the word."

"It sounds sexy," Alex said. "Say *psychosexual* five times fast," and she tried to do it herself but sissed out.

Suki said, "I am not doing very well in my classes. I

am not going to finish in style, as Miss Brigham says."
Suki said, "I want to goof off more than ever."

Marlene

Marlene would like to explain to Astra Dell why she
had taken some of Astra's letters from Car. How she had
wanted to know what it felt like to be Car Forestal.
Once home, each letter shriveled like a trick every
time—just a hankie from a hat, who cared? Nothing
was changed; Marlene was still herself. She read one of
the filched letters again. It was not loving. *People make
the most impact on the lives of others by being absent.* Not so
true. Her father had left her mother. Marlene was at
school when he packed the yellow cardboard suitcase
her mother remembered him carrying. Marlene's father
had left her mother a hundred years ago. His name was
Bob. As far as she was concerned, her father was just a
stupid name that didn't send money. Marlene's grandmother, Aunt Ruth and Uncle Ted, her cousins Wendy
and Steven, all relatives on her mother's side, were coming to Marlene's graduation. In the drawing for pews,
Marlene had drawn seats from the middle of the church.
Astra Dell was also in the middle of the church. Car
Forestal was in the front.

Beyond Astra Dell, Marlene and Car Forestal had

this in common: Their families were small; their fathers were absent.

Unattached

"I didn't want him to take an interest in my leaving New York. Of course, I didn't, Mother."

Tim Weeks had said the River School would be lucky to have her. He said he would be sorry to see Anna go but that he understood.

But what exactly was it that he understood? Did he know how disappointed she was not to have persuaded him to regard her beyond the status of a colleague? Did he understand that part of the winter's experience? A seven-month winter, October to May.

CHF

The easiest way to get the figure you want is to be sick. That was a sick thought, but she had thought it more than once. She drank a cup of bitter coffee and decided not to call him. *Too much French pastry, Carlotta:* her father, in front of the slender Dutch hostess, who knew so many languages. French, chief among them—

APs. The tests, the tests were coming up, and was she ready?

Unattached

The middle-school girls were shushing about boys in whispers. *When I liked him and he liked me; he she he she.* Other words came through—*knew* and *asked* and *kissed*—in the conversation Anna Mazur overheard as study-hall proctor. The only other stand-out words, before she told them to be quiet, were *french fries* and *breath.* The school conspired against her: Last-period study hall every other Friday in spring was a cruel assignment, especially today. Today she was meeting Tim Weeks for a walk in the park—her request.

She wanted to give him something to remember her by, but she had to proceed furtively, out of school, or else—and this made no sense she knew but she thought it—her mother would find out and tell her it was another stupid move. Women don't give men presents.

Maybe not, but Anna Mazur had a present for Tim Weeks in her bag, and it made her happy to see him walking toward her down the hall when she had a surprise for him. But they were not yet out of school. Lower-school dismissal was begun, and they craned over the stairwell from just above to watch the little girls jangle down the stairs, little walking packages, projects strapped to their backs. Some looked stunned, some sealed, still others tickled to death. "What was school like for you?" She had asked him this question before, and he had answered in the same way then as now. School was messy and unfinished, full of guilt. He was shy—largely mute—but physically way ahead of everybody his age. "I was faster. The gap diminished as we got older, but in elementary school I could run circles around my classmates, and I was treated specially. I was picked first for teams. I didn't have to talk to make my way among kids." Most of school was a sunny tedium, but there were flashes when Tim Weeks felt himself reverse the flow of the game, intercept, drive the ball. "You can be the most closed person, yet if you are an athlete and in that world, junior high school, you are part of the social scene. I eventually worked for the school playgrounds, coaching baseball. I've been teaching kids since I was seventeen. Never had to live in the adult world."

He said, "But I have a tremendous sympathy for those who don't have the same ease with life."

Anna Mazur was one of these and uncomfortable in life, which might explain the pleasure she felt in Tim Weeks's company. How, walking with him now on the bridle path around the reservoir, she felt favorably observed by strangers, approved, envied, light on her feet. Anything she had to say seemed of interest to him; he listened; he laughed. Was she really funny? She hoped so!

"Here," she said, and she took out of her bag a silver-plated personalized bar to hold open books and, tasseled as it was, to serve as a bookmark. She had had his initials and the school year engraved on one side. (For a time she debated something else, his initials and her own initials, her first name?)

"Annie," he said. "How nice of you! But this wasn't necessary." He hugged her. He said, "I am going to miss you next year."

Really? she silently asked, and the voice she heard was Gillian Warring's saying, *Do you miss us? Do you like the present sixes better than you liked us?*

It was so easy to flatter a teacher. *I hope I have you next year.*

Anna Mazur and Tim Weeks stood downwind of a poignant scent—was it verbena? "I'm going to miss you," she said. "This year has been very eventful, what with Astra Dell and all, and you've made it a heck of a lot easier. You listened to me about my brother and my mother and the English department, Hodd and O'Brien—all of that." So Anna Mazur was professing love to a man who had yet to kiss her with any romantic intention. "I'm really grateful," she said. Her tongue stuck in her mouth.

"Oh"—his response—"I was glad to listen." He said he had learned a lot about *Jane Eyre* that he never knew. Mr. Rochester in disguise was far more dangerous than ever Tim Weeks suspected. Tim said, "We've had fun," and he turned his body in a way that was welcoming but in a forward direction, not toward her, but continuing along the path. "Walk with me," he said, when what she heard was *This is why I can't.* The story he went on to tell had to do with his home, and a hometown girl, and their being rumored into romance—one of the reasons he decided to strike out on his own in New York. "I don't want to be in a position of making anyone unhappy," he said.

Prizes

Unattached

"That's all he said, Mother."

Once Tim Weeks had thought to join the ministry, but he had majored in history instead. He was a sixth-grade history teacher at the Miss Siddons School. Some years he had taught eighth-grade history. Astra Dell had been his student. She reminded her mother of just who Astra Dell was, but her mother cut in.

"I know," her mother said. "The sick girl."

Anna Mazur hugged a cushion. "I'm depressed, Mother, is what it is." Beyond the cloudy window, the river insinuated itself, seeming scaly as a snake and the same dirty brown. This, whatever this was, whatever she had known with Tim Weeks while Astra Dell was sick, was a flirtation. Tim Weeks was as serious about Anna as he was about Gillian Warring. Tim Weeks was the school's bachelor. There were actually three of them that she knew of, but Tim Weeks was nearer her age and so very cute. She was a type, too, common as a robin, a Miss forever in a Miss Siddons School. In Miss

Brigham's office was a portrait photograph of Margaret Witt Siddons, founder, 1921: a barefaced woman from an old-fashioned time. Everything, the picture seemed to say, is gone, everything but the desk and the modern version of Miss Siddons, a head of school who was not above wearing a pantsuit in cold weather.

Marlene

Marlene Kovack was working backstage in costumes for social service hours when she overheard someone—too loud—a middle schooler, say, "You know when people are gay, don't you?" Mr. Weeks was nearby, with props, and she wondered, as she wondered about many of the unattached faculty in school, but why were the middle schoolers always so out of control? Marlene helped only the lower schoolers in the play. The lower schoolers were delicate and shy; they made peeping sounds as Marlene dressed them, the King of Siam's littlest children.

Francesca Fratini swung into the room and cooed over the King of Siam's two littlest children. "Oh, don't you look pretty. I love your headdresses." Then to Marlene, "Remember when we were this size?"

The little girls had hands as small as starfish. "How old are you again?" Marlene asked, and the little girls answered: first grade. Marlene said, "I was never this small in first grade."

Francesca said to Marlene, "You should come to the interschool *Macbeth*. I'm one of the witches. Our director is crazy. I have to lick Macbeth's face like a dog."

The King of Siam's littlest children turned in their seats to look at Francesca Fratini. "Am I scaring you?" she said. "That's the kind of thing you get to do in high school. I'm a senior." Francesca said, "What do you think of that?"

Little shrugs from the little rouged girls, who stepped away lightly as if their feet were bound.

"You scared them," Marlene said.

"Look, Marlene," and Francesca turned around, and there was a bumper sticker on her butt: *Property of the King of Siam.* "Prank night," she said. "When we all bow and our hoop skirts flip up, this is what the King and Anna will see!"

Marlene stayed for the cast party and ate cake and went downtown with Francesca Fratini and Gillian Warring, who were doing their imitations of Dr. Bell. They called him the stress doctor and said he came to Siddons twice a week to get the kinks out. Their story was Dr. Bell had an office in the basement at school and that only the nurse had a key. "She takes us downstairs and lets us in," Francesca said.

"He helps you with all the ways you're backward," Gillian said. "I can't believe you don't know this. I know this, and I am in eighth grade!"

Marlene said, "It's an extra, probably, like tutoring."

"No," Francesca said, "you just have to reverse your letters to be in the club."

Dr. Bell had a mustache, and when he spoke, spit caught on the bristles of his mustache and it was gross. It was a mustard color, too—dirty mustard. "It makes me sick," Gillian said. "He has terrible breath, and he sits too close and watches you read for speed, and he keeps his pencil near when you write, and he corrects you as you go along, and you get all confused and of course you seem dumb to him. You're dumb to yourself. The man makes you dumb." Gillian took up Francesca's hands and danced with her the way the King did with Anna. "God! I hate him! Dr. Bell . . ." After a few turns, Gillian stopped short and confided to Marlene, "Can you tell I've been drinking?" One of the beauties of school was in its bringing like minds together briefly and intensely in these moments outside of school. Now in the Village outside a bar that blinked at fake IDs, Marlene held Gillian's hair while she puked into the street. Francesca went back in the bar to buy the drunk girl a Coke.

A Daughter

"I've just been here too long," Lisa Van de Ven said to Miss Wilkes. "I can't get interested in a single subject. I don't like anyone in my class. Nothing. The other day

three of the nine seniors in AP French showed up." Lisa
Van de Ven said, "I can't wait to get out of here." Then
she said *college* as if she were making a wish, and she
shut her eyes. "That's what I'm passionate about, if you
want to know. Leaving. I can't wait."

Youth in its sullen husk, dry, shrunk, ugly as a corn-
stalk, prematurely autumnal, an awful, rasping wasteful-
ness, Lisa Van de Ven tamped her bloody thumb with a
napkin and talked about how alienated she felt from all of
her classmates. "Ever since the Dance Concert," Lisa said
to her, and said again, "I can't wait to get out of here."
She did not look up at Miss Wilkes until the end of recess,
and for a moment it seemed to the woman that the girl's
face signaled something other than complaint. Was Lisa
embarrassed, for Miss Wilkes was certainly embarrassed.
However could she have cared so much about this tough
girl, but she had; she hoped Lisa Van de Ven would stop
chewing her thumb long enough to look up again and see
the expression on her teacher's face, an expression that
felt easy and dispassionate in its perfect insincerity. "Soon
enough you'll be gone," Miss Wilkes said, "but you'll be
missed. You must promise to come back and visit us."

Unattached

"Happy in this, she is not yet so old / But she may learn;
happier than this, / She is not bred so dull but she can

learn." Portia to Bassanio at the English Speaking Union Shakespeare contest, 1995. Anna Mazur had coached her in Miss Hodd's stead. (Poor Miss Hodd had been sick then.) Anna Mazur had coached Astra Dell, and Astra Dell had remembered the speech as well as the sonnet. One of their chief topics of conversation in the hospital had been Shakespeare and what plays Astra Dell knew and liked best. Her favorite was *A Midsummer Night's Dream*, which wasn't original, Astra knew, but Anna Mazur said, of course, it was a favorite of hers, too.

Favorites. Anna Mazur wanted to be a favorite.

"See what a memory she has!" Anna Mazur said to Tim Weeks.

"I heard," Tim Weeks said, and he saw how small Astra was, shrunk a little, her long sleeves loose over her hands, only fingertips visible. He stood with Miss Mazur and watched as Astra walked down the hall to her next class.

Anna Mazur said, "Her hair, at least it's growing. I almost said 'glowing.'"

Suki and Alex

The prom was in the future, along with a lot of other ceremonies from which someone would walk home with a corsage or a scroll or a secret-society pin. "I'd hoped to be invited," Suki said. Carlotta Forestal, Elizabeth Freer, and Katherine Johnson were the new inductees from the senior class to Cum Laude, the high school equivalent of Phi Beta Kappa; seniors made members in their junior year were Ufia Abiola, Sarah Saperstein, and Ny Song. A cardiologist, Siddons, class of '72, addressed the assembly. The cardiologist, at the beginning of her talk, asked if Siddons seniors still had the tea party with the headmistress in the Conservatory Garden.

*No*s from the audience.

Suki said to Alex, "So this person I hardly know asks me if I'm on Wellbutrin. I want to know what about me screams I really require heavy-duty antidepressants." Something the cardiologist said—death? "All year it's been doctors. Astra's still not out of the woods, you know." Suki said, "Get me on Astra's video after this is over. I have something to say."

Siddons

Tea parties with the headmistress. *Headmistress*, that was a word from years ago.

"Too bad," Miss Hodd said, "it's prettier than *head of school*."

"You can't have it both ways," Mr. O'Brien said.

"I'm contradictory. I like the white dresses for graduation, too," Miss Hodd said.

"The girls should be in academic robes," Mr. O'Brien said.

"Oh," Miss F joined in, "white dresses."

"Comme une jeune fille," Madame Sagnier said.

Alex and Suki

Suki smoldered at the camcorder, and Alex turned it off. "I thought you had something to say."

"I thought I did, too, but Astra's being back has taken the punch out of this video." She considered. "I'm glad, of course. Did I sound like my mother just then?" Suki's mother said that most of what was true about human nature was ugly, and Suki cited, as an instance, the fact that Marlene Kovack had visited Astra Dell more than any of Astra's real friends. Marlene, who was not in most of Astra's classes, took it on herself to bring Astra's homework to the hospital.

Marlene

At graduation rehearsal the upper-school chorus bludgeoned "For the Beauty of the Earth" with its high notes never reached: "Lord of all, to thee we raise . . ." But the singing improved with "Jerusalem," and its familiar opening, "And did those feet in ancient time / Walk upon England's mountains green?" Lilies and smokestacks were the hymn's earliest associations for Astra Dell, next came images of Oxford and summer abroad and students in spinnakered capes blown down the High Street. Marlene sat next to Astra Dell in the church and considered Astra's view of the hymn and what Astra was saying about scones and clotted cream and being hungry—"You can't imagine how good it feels," Astra said. To be hungry and here in the church where they would graduate in two days. Astra was graduating. "There won't be a diploma until after I take exams, but then." Astra smiled. A small part of her had learned to keep what hopes she had to herself.

"I understand what you're saying," Marlene said, but she, herself, had changed. That night, with Francesca Fratini and Gillian Warring, when Gillian drank too much and was sick on the curb and Marlene tended to her, that night marked the start of something for Marlene. She began to wear her own accomplishment: a red sweatshirt with a perky badger across her chest. Marlene was going to Mad-town and she felt ready for the multitudes, but, first, she was looking forward to a summer of other nights, just like the one with Francesca and Gillian, nights with friends, confessions, and dramas.

Not everyone was working every day. She wasn't! And she didn't start for another week, and the day after tomorrow she would be released, free! One of forty seniors from the class of 1997, Marlene would walk down the aisle of the church wearing a white A-line satin dress—not exactly summery, but a white dress that might serve a couple of occasions was hard to find— and a seed pearl necklace. And her hair? She pinned her hopes on the hairstylist; otherwise, she was wearing a helmet. Astra, Astra Dell was sitting next to her with her feathery scalp against the back of the pew, looking up, and the blue life-stuff at her temples seemed especially complicated and close to the surface.

Be real.

Marlene took out the journal and wrote. *Be real. Don't ever become fake like the people that say hello in the elevator.* The journal she had started for Astra, a log of lounge events, had long ago turned into something private, though she often wrote in public. She made promises to her self. *I hope that years from now you won't look at this journal and skim it like a dream and laugh and read lines out loud to others. Remember it wasn't about the grades . . . live that way always, it's so much more worth it. Remember the days in the lounge, the music, the classes.* Now her heart was caught up in Astra. *I hope the girl I love now is not one of those fake people. I hope her magic lasts because of her humanity. I hope I wasn't in love with an idea.*

Siddons

Mr. Dell had been at Prize Day every year for the past six years when prizes were first given out to students. Siddons pins and sports letters, all-around everything prizes—*It's in the handbook,* Grace had said. Year after year, perfect attendance, no school day missed until Grace died. Astra wasn't winning a prize this year, but Mr. Dell had come to the occasion to take Astra and Car out to lunch afterward, and when he saw Mrs. Forestal on the other side of the balcony, he knew Car was winning a prize, and that perhaps Mrs. Forestal might join them for lunch. Nice-enough woman, albeit seemingly bewildered and certainly expensive, she was very attractive in a slightly brittle way. He knew men who went in for that precision. Around him now were parents, some from his daughter's class and the Mortons' party. Dr. and Mrs. Saperstein, Mrs. Abiola. The Decrows! Some girls dared to look up at the balcony while others looked straight ahead at the long table with its pile of books in white paper, red ribbons.

Middle- and upper-school faculty sat in the choir stalls; however, Miss Mazur was late and so was Mr. Weeks. They stood in the back and watched for an hour and forty-five minutes as girls in perfect uniform—white shirt, pleated skirt, knee-highs, dark shoes—walked toward the ministerial center of the church to accept prize after prize, named and unnamed. Car Forestal, the Selfridge Prize, for four years of excellence in English. This came as no surprise, except that Astra Dell would surely have been in the running had she been well and in school all year.

She was well now, wasn't she? Anna Mazur was uncertain. Her brother had died, remember. Yes.

Yes, Car, Car Forestal. Most of the named prizes went to seniors. Sarah Saperstein won the Milton Weiner Science Prize. Her friend Ny, the Dr. Jerome Kronenberg Mathematics Prize. Ufia Abiola won the Sophia Mutti Modern Languages Prize; Kitty Johnson, the William Wadsley Essay Prize, for an essay on *King Lear* she wrote in the spring.

Somehow Alex Decrow had managed to work a rainbow chiffon scarf about her hair, and it fluttered in her rushed walk to accept a prize for improvement in physical education. Was the prize a joke? Alex could hardly breathe for smoking! Seniors in the front row laughed. The scarf and the prize and how she put it past them.

"Mostly, it was attitude," Alex explained after Prize Day was over.

Lisa Van de Ven said to no one in particular in the exiting throng, "I want to do something with my life."

"Speak for yourself," Suki said—to Lisa?

Unattached

Tim Weeks said, "Alex Decrow's prize in PE, who would have guessed?"

Anna Mazur took a packet of Kleenex from her purse and pulled out one, two, three Kleenexes and blew into the bunch of them.

"Anna," he said, "I think I have disappointed you, and I am sorry."

"Oh," she said, "it's just the end of the school year is all."

Gillian Warring, sprung from out of nowhere with silly intentions, took Tim Weeks by surprise. "If it weren't for you," the girl said. Her headband was sliding backward and off, and filaments of colorless hair stood up around her face. The girl was rosy and pretty, a plinging string of a girl with life and more life. She was smiling at Tim Weeks, who held up his arms as if ambushed but smiled and told the girl how he knew, he wasn't surprised, and the girl might have talked longer but for friends—and her parents!

"I never thought Gillian had any parents," Anna Mazur said, then, "Oh, that was bitchy of me," and she cried.

Tim Weeks pulled her out of the crowd and in a corner of the vestibule told her he was stoned. He was too stoned for any of this.

So the pixilated face was a card trick. "You're not naturally cheerful and loquacious?"

He might have elaborated, but he had elaborated. More than once Tim Weeks had admitted he liked teaching middle school, and he liked teaching at Siddons. Beyond the school's doors was for him vacancy, silence, sickness. Beyond the doors the women he knew in school changed; conversations were full of holes; nothing felt finished but about to begin and about to begin, and then of course it didn't; he stalled. This did not mean Tim Weeks could not feel love; he could—he did. He felt affection for many people. "Do you want to know why I think I'm successful at this work? It's because I'm their age; I think the way a twelve-year-old might think. Look inside any school and you'll find characters like me, Anna. Like most teachers, I'm more comfortable around kids than grown-ups. I like them better. I have more to say to them. And middle school. Kids are at their funniest then. Middle school is the best part of school." The way the girls slung themselves against objects and other people; the way they bruised and healed so quickly.

"Middle school," Tim Weeks said in a voice that sounded like a lover's. Rough expressions he had heard could be beautiful. *What do you look like on the inside without any clothes?*

Siddons

"Are you still in a snit about the white dresses?" Miss Hodd wanted to know.

"Edith Wharton would not approve," Mr. O'Brien said. "Poor Edith! She was left to learn at home with a governess, you'll recall, and the really good books were forbidden her in her father's library . . ."

Mr. Gates, Mrs. Archibald, Mr. Quinn and Mr. Santiago and Mr. Johnston, Mrs. Riley, Dr. Meltzer, Jade, who taught dance, Mr. Principia, Rose, Denny, and Jorge, from the cooking staff, Mariana Papadakios, who costumed plays, and Miss Barns, who directed them, the math team, Phil and Judy, the librarians, Lucy Caldwater and Helena Miser and Mrs. Cohen, the entire physical education department, swimming downstream, en masse, Bilba, from the music department, and Peter Hoy, who ran technology, were some of the guests on their way to the fancy faculty luncheon. Mr. Carson, Señora Valdez, and Anna Mazur were one group walking up Madison Avenue. Tim Weeks had told Anna Mazur he would be there just as soon as he was finished signing yearbooks.

Mrs. Van de Ven explained she had come early for a back-row seat where she would not be seen by the girls marching in, and there she had discreetly sat through

Prize Day. She had come not because Lisa was winning a prize—Lisa was not, Mrs. Van de Ven knew it or she would have been called—but Mrs. Van de Ven had come to applaud the entire senior class and their teachers for their efforts and accomplishments. "And your daughter," Mrs. Van de Ven said to Mr. Dell, "your daughter is here. That's wonderful."

Her *wonderful* sounded hollow to him, though Mr. Dell could appreciate the sound of disappointment: how to explain Lisa's empty arms on June 11, 1997? Lisa was graduating, was going to . . . where was she going to? Astra hadn't said and Mrs. Van de Ven did not say, which seemed to Mr. Dell unlike Lettie Van de Ven, but he thanked her for her solicitous inquiries about his daughter. Astra was well; they were in holding mode, but she was well. She would be walking with her class.

"Yes, of course," Mrs. Van de Ven said, "I know." Mrs. Van de Ven was a class rep, so she knew; she knew a lot that was happening at school. Certainly, she knew about Astra. "Does she ever wear that wig you bought her?"

"She may have," he said. "I don't know."

Mrs. Van de Ven said, "There's so much we don't know about our children, isn't there?" These were the last days, weren't they? Never again high school, this school. Yes to the campaigns and annual funds, yes to the ten-year reunions, but never again this daily abrasion: the wonder it was possible to feel so much. Didn't

Mr. Dell think that was so? Her own daughter had ruined her thumbnails with nervous sucking. "Some nights I thought to myself, she's just a baby." Then there was the club scene after spring vacation, the slacking off—the terrible slacking off—the smell of cigarettes in the clothes tossed about the room. Messy stacks of homework for weeks unmoved, untouched, and new books, novels from the spring electives—Families in Distress (poor choice)—their spines unbroken. "It's been hard," Mrs. Van de Ven said. "Honestly, I haven't known what to do, and Bill hasn't been any help. He flees to the office and stays late. We haven't had a dinner together, the three of us, in months it feels like. Not since the new year." Mrs. Van de Ven stood with Mr. Dell, who could have left her—she didn't have him in a corner—but he stayed to console her because she had started to cry.

"Tears of joy!" she insisted. "I'm going to miss my little girl."

CHF

That day was the last day I lived in my body. I retreated above the neck, and I've lived inside the "fire" in my head ever since. This was not the first time Car recognized herself in a play, although it was the first time she heard her own feelings expressed in the same images she had used all winter to describe the fever that was hardly purgatorial but a low-grade, constant wearing away. *Nobody wakes up in the morning trying to burn.*

Car walked Astra to her building, where they talked on the corner out from under the stage light of the iron-and-glass marquee. The play had been Astra's idea, but Car had known what it was about: a girl and her uncle in a car. What is it about uncles and fathers, Car wanted to know. "Have you ever loved somebody so intensely that you wanted to be inside them—literally, you wanted to slide down their throat? Something out of sci-fi, I know, but I'm serious, I've felt this way about my father. I've felt it for him and he's felt it for me, I'm sure, but then last spring. And now I haven't seen him in over a year. He comes to New York when I'm away with Mother. I went to his apartment the other day. I still have the key. I'd left the place a mess. I thought, let it look lived-in, let him see I've been here, but the other day—and I know he's got help—the place had been cleaned up, and there were no signs of me, but there were signs of him. I know. I know him. I know he was in New York." Car let herself be embraced, although it was easier to cry outside of someone's arms, and she did want to cry a little more. "It feels good to cry," she said. "There was a time last year when I thought I'd run out of the power to cry."

"I know," Astra said, "but you haven't."

"Oh, Astra," Car said. "I know I go on and on about my own problems, but I do love you, and I'm so glad we're just standing here." She saw the moment in Astra: the new green that glowed in the border along the staunch building. "You better promise to visit next year."

"Car."

"I was the one, you know," Car said. "He didn't do anything really. He wouldn't. I mean, you know my father when he's had too much to drink." If she could only describe the way his body strained its casing. "Do you remember years ago that sleepover I had when he came home and stepped on Kitty Johnson?"

"Oh my."

"That's the way he is. He gets very sad, goes out and drinks, and comes home walloped and stumbles around until he finds something soft to lie on."

"It's been a long time since I've seen your father," Astra said. "Mom's funeral, I think."

"Astra . . ."

"No, it's all right. I'm fine. I talk to Mom all the time, and I know she hears me. That sounds silly, but it's true. Sometimes when I was sick, I was sure she was sitting on my bed."

"It's not silly."

"I know you, Car," then, "Mom says hi. She says, 'Embrace the world.'" Astra took her friend's arm, said, "Come on. It's okay."

"That was a heavy-duty play tonight."

"Yes, it was. Come on," Astra said. "I'll walk you." This, their habit from whenever it was they were first allowed to walk home alone or together. Car would walk Astra to her apartment building, then Astra would turn and walk Car back to hers just to keep talking, but they had never before fallen into quite such a silence. It felt like what Car imagined was marriage.

Fathers

This year two trends in the tulip plantings along Park Avenue: Either the tulips were tight and fringed, or else they were sloppy, enormous, the size of soup bowls in very bright yellows and oranges; on the streets, red. The plantings along the buildings on Fifth Avenue in the Nineties had more interest for Wendell Bliss. These plantings he saw as a response to the park on the other side; they were done up in a woodsy way, oak-leaf hydrangea, hellebores, and bulbs—grape hyacinth, daffodils, and proportionate white tulips. The borders at night looked watered and cool, and Mr. Bliss watched Peanut for signs, but tonight the little dog seemed happy only to be out, and she minced along just ahead. Her "mother" was home now that Marion Bliss was home. Marion was home, and her mother and the long ordeal of winter were past. Poor Marion. *I keep on expecting my mother to call.*

The girl walking toward Wendell Bliss looked almost as sad as his wife. Beautiful girl, she seemed to rearrange herself with a shake as she passed, but she passed by so quickly he couldn't return her small hello.

Acknowledgments

I wish to thank Rev. Alison B. Miller, whose fortitude and grace when confronting just such a cancer as Astra Dell's inspired this novel. Astra Dell's college essay quotations and her "Yes" to life attitude are taken from Rev. Miller's sermon "Leap of Faith." Astra Dell, however, is an entirely fictional character and all details of her life, as well as the Siddons School, its community, and their actions, are invented.

For the gift of time, as well as support and affection, thank you to Dorothy Hutcheson, Laura Kirk, John Loughery, Abby Weintraub, and Elizabeth Hartley Winthrop.